Walt S

THE
LIVELY
DEAD

THE LIVELY DEAD

Peter Dickinson

Pantheon Books, New York

Copyright © 1975 by Peter Dickinson

All rights reserved under International and Pan-American Copyright Conventions. Published in the United States by Pantheon Books, a division of Random House, Inc., New York. Originally published in Great Britain by Hodder and Stoughton Limited.

Library of Congress Cataloging in Publication Data

Dickinson, Peter, 1927–
The Lively Dead.

  I. Title.
PZ4.D5525Lg3 [PR6054.I35] 823'.9'14 74-25226
ISBN 0-394-73317-7

Manufactured in the United States of America

First Pantheon Paperback Edition 1982

THE LIVELY DEAD

1

BENDING TO ADJUST THE CLAW of her crowbar against a joist, Lydia saw the man's feet. The Building Inspector from the Borough Council, she thought, come about that beam and high time too. She didn't turn round because it amuses most men to see a woman struggling with a man's work, and consequently it amused Lydia to startle them. She heaved firmly on the crowbar and relished the mandrake-screech as the nails came up that vital first quarter-inch.

Then she worked along the board, using the crowbar in her right hand and the claw-hammer in her left. It came out more cleanly than some. If it wasn't infected she could use it again. She flipped it over on its back above the cavity and worked along it with the hammer, banging the nails half-way out so that she could turn it over once more and claw them free. A male workman would have let them fall into the cavity, but Lydia collected them in an old coffee-tin, not because they were any use but because she didn't like the idea of bent and rusty nails littered below her floor. When at last she looked up, pretending to notice him for the first time, she found it was not a bloke from the Council but a gentleman from the Government—little Mr Obb, currently Minister of Maritime Affairs, waiting there dapper and sad.

"I interrupt, I fear," he said.

"I'm in a bit of a hurry," said Lydia. "If I don't get the floor back down before I fetch Dickie he'll insist on exploring the whole cavity, and get stuck probably and filthy certainly. I don't really mind him getting dirty, except that it's not too easy to clean him up again at the moment."

Mr Obb smiled, but even that was sad. He was a small, freckled, shiny old man with very pale eyes. The dust and the dank odour from the cavity and the dreary light from the bare bulb seemed like a stage atmosphere, created to enhance his central melancholy. Bloody hell, thought Lydia. He wants me to do something.

"It is not nice to be stuck under floors," he said. "I have hidden for five weeks in much such a place, under a cabin in the woods. The ground was marshy so that my clothes rotted off my limbs. Only I did not rot."

"Is something the matter, Mr Obb?"

"Yes, yes. The duplicator will not function."

As Lydia rose from her knees echoes of that first "bloody hell" diminished down the tunnels of her resentment. But it probably wouldn't take ten minutes, and it might be useful to see what sort of a mess the Government were making of their rooms since Mrs Newbury had died.

"OK, I'll see what I can do," she said, beginning to peel off the rubber gloves and kick off her wellingtons at the same time.

"Have I behaved carelessly, coming down here in ordinary clothes?" asked Mr Obb.

"It's all right," said Lydia, slipping her feet into her Scholl sandals. "There's a lot of mumbo-jumbo about dry rot—the spores are all over the place anyway, so it doesn't make much difference if you spread a few more around. What matters is leaving infected timber about. I wear these things to keep myself in decent nick. Shall I go first?"

The Government occupied the top two floors of the five-storey house in Devon Crescent, W.11, of which Lydia was the landlord. They had their own brass plate and bell at the front door, and again at the inner door at the bottom of the flight up to the fourth floor. By the time they reached this point Mr Obb was gasping with the climb, so that Lydia knew that despite her hurry she'd have to stop and let him rest. Poor old boy, she thought; he'd already been something in the Livonian Government when the Russians had taken over the Baltic States in 1940; say he'd been fortyish then, he must be well over seventy now. But even a septuagenarian male face has to be saved, if possible. She nodded towards Mrs Newbury's door, on the right of the landing.

"Have you found a new cleaner yet?" she asked. "You'll miss Mrs N."

"We are interviewing candidates," said Mr Obb, a little distantly, as if wishing to imply that the engagement of a charlady was an Internal and not a Maritime Affair.

"It won't be the same, I'm afraid," said Lydia. "She was very fond of you."

"A good servant. To such people one has obligations."

Again, despite the panting, Lydia heard a tone of mild reproof, as if Mr Obb didn't admit the relationship of "fondness" between master and servant. Silly old driveller, she thought, but her impatience with him was suddenly exorcised by his sweet smile.

"We have made all arrangements for the funeral," he said.

"Yes, I know. It's very kind of you."

"It will be in the Liv fashion. The coffin comes here to-day, at noon."

"Back here!" Lydia claimed to be squeamish not about death itself but about the trappings and fuss of burial.

"That is our fashion. I understand that she had no kin except this daughter who is in prison, so it is for us to sit and watch with the body while the Long Candle burns and the soul goes to God. Then to-morrow is the burial. You will attend?"

Lydia shrugged. It was the last thing she wished to do, but she was grateful to the old man for taking all this on. Almost her first thought when she was coming out of the shock of Mrs Newbury's death had been that she'd have to find the cash to give her even a half-decent funeral, such as she'd longed for, and that would mean cutting down on the plasterer's wages and doing some of the plastering herself, which would have been infuriating as Lydia knew she couldn't do it up to professional standards. And then Mr Obb had taken over. So she could hardly refuse to attend the dreary ceremony.

"Of course I'll come," she said. "And I'll ring up the prison and see if they'll let the daughter out."

"Excellent," said Mr Obb after a slight pause. "I understand she is very beautiful."

Panting no longer he fished a key out of his waistcoat, opened the door and led the way up.

Lydia had never discovered whether all Livonians were mechanical morons, or whether it was just a coincidence that the members of the Government were. Their Gestetner was a servant almost as old as Mrs Newbury and no less faithful, but they treated it without respect. One small error and they panicked, twiddling knobs at random and when that failed applying extra ink to the rollers. The gaunt, grey widows who did their typing would not go near the machine. Lydia, soon after she had bought the house, had come in on one of these scenes of grimy desperation and had sorted things out for

9

them. Since then they had tended to come down about once a month to ask for help.

This time heaps of crumpled paper lay around, streaked with great black lines round the edges. General Busch was standing by the window, tense as a weightlifter, as though making up his mind to throw up the sash and leap to oblivion. Count Linden was kneeling amid the mess, apparently praying. Lydia cleaned up the roller, reset the spacers and eased the stencil smooth. As she adjusted the pile of paper in the rack she saw what was wrong.

"This isn't duplicating paper," she said. "You can't use this."

Mr Obb translated. General Busch swung round from the window with his great slab of a face frowning and his pale eyes glaring at Lydia. He spoke in Livonian.

"The Prime Minister insists that we use that paper," said Mr Obb. "It is high quality paper, for respect. Aakisen is dead."

"Dead!" said Lydia.

"The President of the Livonian Republic is dead," said Mr Obb. "It will be in your newspapers to-morrow, if you can make the duplicator function. The Muscovites have never admitted that they captured him, but we knew. And now further news has reached us. He died two months ago at a camp in Sredne Vilyuysk in Siberia. Only now can we announce this horrible murder to the world. But we must use dignified paper."

"I'm sorry," said Lydia.

She thought of Mrs Newbury and her horror of a pauper's funeral. She thought of these old men, hearing that their national hero, their Churchill-figure, was dead at last, but still finding time and reserves of decency to see that their servant was buried with respect.

"OK," she said, sighing. "I'll see what I can do."

Each sheet needed to be fed individually into the machine. The ink supply had to be exactly right, because the paper was barely absorbent. For the same reason each sheet had to be separately lifted clear and draped somewhere to dry. At first Lydia wasted two sheets in three, but two hours later she had got the ratio down to one in three, and then the job was done. She was dead beat, far more than if she had spent the morning heaving up floor-boards.

"We are truly grateful," said Mr Obb, shirt-sleeved and streaked with ink, but smiling still.

"Varotnisho!" shouted General Busch.

Count Linden, lean and wispy and grey as a mouse's belly, hobbled next door and came back with a heavy decanter and four small tumbler-shaped glasses. The liquid was paler than cider. Lydia sniffed her tot with curiosity and caution, and found it smelt like a milder version of the solvent used in her dry-rot fungicide.

"Aakisen!" snapped General Busch, making the name sound like a snuff-taker's sneeze.

"Aakisen," said the other three, Lydia a little late. The men downed their tots at a gulp. Lydia sipped. As her eyes unblurred she saw swimmingly before her the last sheet she had printed.

AAKU AAKISEN DEAD
President of Livonia, Hero and Patriot,
dies in secret Siberian Labour Camp.
After seventy-six years of fighting and suffering for his
country, the great Aaku Aakisen is dead at last.
The hero who, from his marshy hide-out among the Baltic
lakes, for nine years defied the might of Stalin's armies, and
who since 1955 . . .

Lydia didn't want to know any of that. It was over. She sipped again at her glass and found that she relished the stuff, fiery but smooth, with a strange, clean, piny flavour.

"I'm afraid I can't drink it at a gulp like you do," she said.

"Good, good," said Count Linden. "That is for men and peasant-women. A lady takes only little sips. I regret that we have no smaller glass."

Hell, thought Lydia, watching the little grey creep serve out another whack to the men, next time I'll get it down in one, and I bloody well won't choke either.

"What is it?" she asked.

"Vodka," said Mr Obb.

"But I thought . . ."

"Muscovite vodka is a liquid designed to make swine drunk without effort," explained Count Linden. "This is the vodka of the Livs. *Varosh*, we call it. It is distilled like vodka, but flavoured with hazel nuts and pine cones and some herbs. Of course . . ."

"Leh dillidyat immish!" snarled General Busch, raising his glass.

"Lady Lydia Timms," echoed Mr Obb and Count Linden.

11

Lydia's own glass was half-way to her mouth before she grasped what they'd said. She felt the tide of blushing race up her neck and encrimson her face. The General, smacking his fat grey lips over his empty glass, bellowed with laughter.

Lydia sipped quickly at her drink to hide her shame and fury, gulped and spluttered but managed to control the explosion without doing the nose-trick.

"We are truly most grateful," she heard Mr Obb saying. "Now we will come and assist you with your flooring."

"No, no!" she gasped, thinking of these old men heaving at crowbars, smashing the boards into unusable splinters, falling between joists and breaking ankles. "It's quite all right. I . . ."

A bell rang.

"The bottom door," said Count Linden.

Lydia slipped round the Gestetner and was at the door before any of them had moved.

"I'm going down anyway," she said, brisk as a March wind. "I'll let them in. If it's anything I can't cope with I'll ring your bell three times. OK? Thank you very much for the *varosh*."

Escape from them made her feel remarkably happy. Or was it the booze? Or some gland switching itself on at random? The wooden soles of her sandals made a lively tap-dance on the stairs. Mrs Pumice's baby was awake and starting to whimper. That's what, thought Lydia, when I've finished with this dreary fungus I'll have another baby. Right. That's settled. She was humming *Pin-Ball Wizard* by the time she opened the door.

The man on the doorstep was dressed all in black.

"At least somebody's happy," he said, and before she could answer turned and waved like a butler summoning a train of footmen. Four other men appeared round the privet hedge, carrying a coffin on their shoulders.

"Know where she goes, Miss?" said the first man. "I was expecting one of them old gents."

"That's all right," said Lydia. "I know where they want it."

Going back up the stairs at the pace of the mourners her sandals sounded like drum-taps.

Mrs. Newbury's room had been shifted round. The bed was against one wall, leaving space in the middle for a trestle table draped with the pink and gold flag of the Livonian Republic. The dressing-table which had once been covered with a hundred hideous knick-knacks was now something like an

12

altar. One enormous coloured candle stood on the floor by the trestle.

"Hello," said the undertaker. "Full military honours! OK, lads, table seems firm. Down. To you a bit, Dave. Fine. Tell the old gents. I'll be on the doorstep to-morrow morning, ten o'clock sharp. Ta ta. We can let ourselves out."

"I'm coming down, as a matter of fact," said Lydia. Some of her suppressed shock and disgust must have crept into her voice and come out as aristocratic chill, because the undertaker's demeanour became noticeably servile as they trooped downstairs. Lydia liked this even less than his previous slightly camp parody of grief, but knew that any attempt to sort out the brief relationship would end in mess.

Down in the basement she fitted the planks back over the cavity and tapped a couple of nails into any that were short enough for Dickie to scrabble up. Then she felt she might as well have lunch, so she went into the front room, which at the moment was the Timmses' bedroom, nursery, living-room, kitchen, workshop and study, and boiled herself a couple of eggs. She had picked up the local Trotskyite rag, *Get Notted*, on her way back from taking Dickie to school, so she was able to perch by the window and dip fingers of brown toast into the egg-yolk while she read a series of flailing attacks on the police, the courts, the Borough Council and the private landlords. There was a writer called Tony Bland who seemed to have a particular gift for the plausible but destructive detail. Food and fervour combined to cheer her spirits, overlaying the gloom of the wasted morning and the coming of the coffin and General Busch's boorish gallantry.

After lunch she rang the prison and pecked away for half an hour at the bleak shell of authority, trying to find a cranny through which she could send her message about the funeral to the human core within. Then there was still an hour before it would be time to fetch Dickie, not enough to do the floor-cavity; nor was there any point in starting on any of the minor jobs in the back room until she'd got the big beam out and seen how far the rot had spread. It would be madness to start mucking around in Dickie's bedroom or here, dismally decayed though both rooms were. Lydia roamed round, stared for a minute at the bedraggled back garden, where the unpruned rose-bed, fuzzy with dead willow-herb, spread itself in gawky gestures. She hated gardening. OK, she thought, I'll go out.

She washed her face in the egg-water, brushed the dust

13

and cobwebs out of her straight, coarse, blue-black hair, dug her sheepskin coat out of one of the polythene sacks in which all their clothes were stored at the moment, and let herself out of the basement door.

The spy was standing on the doorstep, sheltering from the faint February drizzle which had begun during lunch. Lydia caught him by surprise, and he her, so neither of them had a story ready. Lydia tended to be sorry for the spies who sometimes hung about Devon Crescent to watch the Government's futile comings and goings; it didn't matter whether they came from Our Side or Their Side; to her they were simply victims of authority, detailed to come and waste a stretch of their own lives.

However a protocol had been established. Richard Timms had begun it, pointing out that if you spoke to a spy as though you had detected his trade he had to report it, and might get punished; the polite thing was to behave and talk as though he had a perfect right to be hanging about, and was engaged on some other business than spying. As some of the spies were probably not spies anyway, this system was doubly good sense.

Lydia's own fictional gift was weak, unlike her husband's, so she preferred to think out a charade beforehand if she knew she was going to meet one of the men. So now she simply looked at him, stammering. He raised his shabby hat. The memory of the horrid rose-bed inspired her.

"Oh," she said, "are you the bloke who was going to come and see about doing the garden for a bit?"

"Uh," said the man. The grunt sounded almost affirmative. Lydia glimpsed a vista of tidy organisation, the rose-bed dug out, the leaves swept up, Mrs Schelling's endless complaints about her back avoided, the spy himself provided with an acceptable mask—but she drew back from the brink. She liked to think things through before she took action.

"I'm afraid I've got to go out now," she said. "Could you come back, let's think, I'll be busy to-morrow morning, and the next day—the day after that? In the morning?"

"Uh," said the man, standing out of her way.

"That's fine," said Lydia and ran up the steps.

She felt full of warmth and inner life. She knew that the sheepskin coat didn't suit her, making her already pudgy figure seem square as a brick. Ages ago, before Dickie was born, one of her half-sister Lalage's blokes had made a family film at Christmas and had shown it to a roomful of people. A

14

lot of it, of course, had been of Lalage looking languorous, but there'd been one long middle-distance take of Lydia walking down a path beside a yew hedge, wearing a heavily padded anorak. The whole room had laughed, including Lydia herself. So now she knew exactly what she looked like as she clip-clopped past the sugar-icing façades of the other Devon Crescent houses—a sort of square leather parcel-thing, with her sturdy legs strutting jerkily below and her aggressive little head, pink-cheeked, black-browed, poking out at the top. She didn't mind. She was herself, Lydia Timms. That's what she *was* like. You could say that the trouble with the sheepskin coat was that it suited her too well.

She went to Minwick's and bought a couple of hacksaw blades and resisted the temptation of a brutal blue wrench which would have been just the job when it came to cope with back-room sink, but at four pounds sixty was simply a luxury, when she could do the job with the tools she had already. Then she went to the hire shop and checked that the Acrow hoists were coming to-morrow afternoon. She came out knowing from the man's manner that they were, but wouldn't have been if she hadn't checked. At the library she looked in vain for something to read to a seven-year-old dyslexic boy who had an obsession with warfare; she also checked the travel shelves to see whether there were any new books on Russia (there were) and whether any of the travellers had thought Livonia worth more than the usual Intourist paragraph (they hadn't).

Finally she picked Dickie up from his remedial tutor, took him to Holland Park for a machine-gun battle with his cronies in the adventure playground, and home for tea.

She was still cheerful.

2

EVEN AT WEEK-ENDS Lydia and Richard Timms didn't speak much to each other during the day, and their week-day evenings, once Dickie was in bed, would have appeared to a stranger very gruff and chilly. If something simply had to be discussed they would talk it over rather formally, like a two-man committe. But mostly after supper Richard worked at his law-books while Lydia made careful diagrams for tomorrow's carpentry, or drew look-and-say pictures of tanks, Greek hoplites, Crecy archers and atomic submarines, or—if she felt suddenly escapist—worked on her plan of the fantasy car she was going to build as soon as Richard was earning real money and the dry rot was vanquished. They had no television and seldom listened to the radio.

But once the lights were out they were both slow droppers-off, and since Richard's breakdown had got into the habit of talking for an hour in the dark, sometimes in each other's arms for a while and then holding hands, but more often simply lying side by side on their backs. When they had to spend a night apart Lydia missed this hour horribly and found it difficult to go to sleep at all. She wondered, those times, whether—supposing Richard took a girl to his hotel room (unlikely)—he simply lay on his back in the dark and talked to *her*. That would have made Lydia more jealous than if he'd attended the sort of orgies at which Procne Newbury had earned her living before she went to jail.

"Dead?" said Richard. "Yes, I suppose it's about time."

"What do you mean? You usually say he doesn't exist."

"Um."

"Then he can't be dead. I mean . . . Don't be flip about it, darling. I can't imagine why, but a care."

"Sorry. What I think I meant is that they'd have to kill him off some time—it'd look a bit fishy if they were still putting out propaganda about the great national hero imprisoned by the wicked Bolsheviks when he was officially a hundred and

16

twenty. They must have slipped a year or two in any case. He can't have been only seventy-six."

"It said seventy-six years of fighting. He couldn't have begun till he was . . . how old?"

"Say twelve. Eighty-eight. Pretty long-lived for a labour camp."

"He existed once."

"Of course. You know, I think he was probably pretty well always a figurehead—that's why they made him President in the first place. Then he stayed behind with the Resistance, and I should think the Russians got him about 1946, tidying up after the war. The people here would simply hope, and go on putting out propaganda stories about him and his Hereward-the-Wake stunt in the marshes. But when the Cold War began to thaw, and Amnesty got going, and so on, they decided that they'd get more mileage out of making him a prisoner of conscience, or whatever they call it, so they announced that news had come that he was in Siberia. But even that couldn't last for ever. Now's a good time to bump him off."

"Why now?"

"Oh, well, they must be getting pretty jumpy now Sir Alec's gone from the FO. He'd invested a lot of face in the Baltic States, right back to before the war, so even with all this détente going on he'd have stood by them. The Kremlin boys never give up. At some point quite soon there'll be something we want, and they'll ask for a quid pro quo, and that might be closing down the Baltic legations in London and recognising Russia's de jure sovereignty—we'd do it, too, if they offered us enough. So all the old men can hope is to up the price by throwing Aakisen into the fight. If people believe he's just been starved to death in a labour camp, it'll make it that bit harder for us to go along with the Russians."

"It makes me sick. If a thing's wrong in the first place, it can't suddenly become right just because we've got a new Foreign Secretary."

"There aren't any rights in that world—only a choice between wrongs."

"I hope it was true—Aakisen, I mean."

"I rather approve of the old boys, fighting their war with men who are dead already and can't be killed any more."

"They brought back Mrs N to-day."

The tenants were none of Richard's business and he had seen very little of Mrs Newbury. He simply accepted the

17

news with a grunt, and it was some seconds before he really took in what Lydia had said.

"Back?" he said.

"The Government are being very funny about her. They've laid out her room like a military chapel, and they're going to stand sentry over it all night."

Richard chuckled.

"I nearly took Dickie up to see," said Lydia.

"Good God! Isn't that carrying his obsessions a bit far?"

"Oh, it wasn't for the soldier bit. It's just I've read you ought to get kids used to the meaning of death. I'm not keeping hamsters."

"Darling, I don't think it's a very good idea."

"I only thought about it. He didn't really like Mrs N. She used to make him kiss her."

"Ugh. That makes it worse. Furry corpse stiffening in its cage, I can see the point. Ogress shut away in box, nightmares. She'd be lifting the lid and coming for him."

Most of Lydia's own nightmares ran at the level of attending grand dinners and discovering she was still wearing her rubber gloves. Only occasionally did she wander into a darker world, and even then it seemed to be someone else who ran, hopeless, from . . . waking, she could not even remember what, only the terror.

"I think I've got a gardener," she said.

"That's housekeeping."

"I think I can scrape up three hours a week. And I was talking to Mr. Tevell at 76, and he hates gardening too. And 87's a jungle—I don't know the people there but I can go and ask. And Jack Stoddart would far rather spend time on that stupid boat of his. And it wouldn't matter if this bloke didn't know anything about gardening because Mrs Schelling would love to boss him about and I know she's looking for somebody because her back is getting so bad."

"Where on earth did you find a man with so much time? What does *he* say?"

"He said 'Uh' twice. I bumped into him in the doorway. He's the latest spy."

"Darling!"

"I can't see why it shouldn't work. And it would give the poor sod something *real* to do."

"I can see you're going to make it work. I love you. You spend half your days fighting social systems and the other half constructing new ones. You're the Lenin of W.11."

Lydia didn't feel like wandering down the old track, endlessly fascinating to Richard, that explored the thicket of her own personality. She didn't find it a very interesting place.

"I wonder how you get references from a spy," she said.

"Supposing he is one."

"Who else could he be, hanging around in the basement door? Oh, bloody hell! You don't think he was the Building Inspector?"

"Inspectors are more garrulous than that."

"Damn! If it wasn't him, he didn't come. I bet he comes when I'm at the funeral."

3

MR OBB, wearing a black frock coat and a black tie, came down to fetch Lydia. His pale eyes widened slightly at the sight of her.

"I'm sorry," she lied. "I haven't got anything blacker than this."

It was a dark blue trouser-suit, ideal for wearing at windy gravesides. Its sharp-edged, soldierly cut looked well on Lydia, emphasising her competence and energy, mitigating her pudginess.

"We will provide a sash," said Mr Obb.

"Thank you."

(The last time Lydia had worn a black sash was outside South Africa House.)

Almost a dozen frock-coated men waited in the hall. Two or three were surprisingly young. At a nod from General Busch they marched out down the steps and peeled off into the glossy black cars of the cortege.

"Have you met Mr Paul Vaklins?" said Mr Obb. "Lady Timms."

Lydia, already shrinking into herself, reducing her world-awareness against the coming dreary charade, took a second to realise that she was being introduced to one of the young men, whom she vaguely recognised. His large, muscular body was topped by a head which seemed slightly too small and not quite adult, as though the years had never properly smoothed out the crumpled skin of childbirth. Apart from that he would have been very handsome, with his short blond hair and pale blue eyes. He half-bowed.

"We've encountered each other a couple of times on the stairs," he said. "I have the honour to escort you, Lady Timms. My car's down here."

He led her to a vast, bright yellow monster, Italian coach-work on an American chassis by the look of it. The door he held for her seemed as big as the whole side of a Mini.

"I'll stay a bit back," he said as the big engine sucked the car away behind the black Daimlers. "She's not quite the thing for a funeral. I hope you don't mind."

"I prefer it," said Lydia. "I love cars. In a year or two I'm going to build one for myself."

One like this?"

"No, almost the exact opposite, as a matter of fact. Small and square, with a very tight lock. Sixty m.p.g. Nothing to rust. My husband says it will be a hundred-mile-an-hour shopping basket."

She cocked her head and listened to the engine.

"Sixteen cylinders?" she asked.

"That's right—it's a bit ridiculous, isn't it? I tell myself it's a symbol of exile. I don't have a home, I have a car."

Lydia warmed to him, not simply because he accepted without a smile the notion that a woman could build her own car. His hands on the steering were stubby and short-fingered and he drove with no fuss at all, although the pace of the cortege came tiresomely at a point where his automatic transmission couldn't quite make up its mind between ratios. At traffic lights the car sidled close up behind the last of the Daimlers.

"Did you ever meet Aakisen?" said Lydia.

He seemed faintly startled, turning to stare at her with ice-blue Livonian eyes. Then he laughed.

"Yes, I see," he said. "You're being a bit subtle, but you may be right. Because we can't bury Aakisen properly we're acting out our mourning by giving a grand funeral to this woman? But no, I never met him. In fact I never heard his name until I came to England. Officially in Russia he didn't exist."

"Oh . . . I didn't realise . . . I mean you speak English so well."

"Better than I speak Liv, to be honest. Russian is my first language and English my second. Liv is a nursery language I've had to re-learn. I got out in the aftermath of the Krushchev regime. But my old colleagues, they stick to their bad accents as a means of sticking to their identities. I think if you shouted at Busch in English that the house was on fire he would run down the stairs."

"I'd like to be there. It sometimes irritates me, I'm afraid, though I'm not much good at languages myself. Is that why they're such mechanical nits, too?"

"Uh?"

"I have to keep running up and mending the Gestetner for them. If you're going to be about at all, I'll show you and you can do it."

"I don't know. I would say that their mechanical incompetence was a bourgeois class thing, a bit like the way Chinese Mandarins grew their nails long to demonstrate that they did no manual work. So gentlemen and intellectuals prefer to show that they do not belong to the mechanic classes. But as for being at Devon Crescent . . . it's not the ideal moment to ask, but have you any plans for Mrs Newbury's room?"

"For you?"

"If possible. There's going to be a Government reshuffle, now Aakisen is dead. Busch will be President and Obb Prime Minister, and I will take over Maritime Affairs. After all, I own the ship."

"I thought there was more than one."

"Yes, there are six, but I own the new one."

"How on earth did you get a new one?"

Lydia knew that some of the Government's money came from the tiny merchant fleet that happened to be out of Livonia when the Russians had come. But by now all of them must surely be much-patched old dodderers.

"Willi Brandt gave it to me, in effect, as a result of his Ostpolitik. It was a highly complex transaction which freed certain assets frozen in East Germany but belonging to me through my grandmother who was a West German. It would take a lawyer to explain how these assets came to me not as cash but in the form of a 6,000-ton Stralsund-built coaster. Do I drive in? Will the car mar the atmosphere of grief? Agh, it is too cold to walk."

In the car-park he helped her to adjust the black sash, again with unfussy efficiency, so much so that he surprised her by standing back when he had finished and saying, "No need to be ashamed of it. It goes with your uniform. The sash of the Order of Aakisen."

She smiled meaninglessly, not even sure whether it was a joke. He took her arm and led her along a muddy gravel driveway behind the old men, bareheaded now, who were following the flower-strewn hearse. The path became worse and worse, puddled, and churned here and there by tyres. Grey grave-stones flanked it, hugger-mugger, the grass between them coarse and spiritless as that on an over-used recreation field. They crossed another driveway, and here the grass was not even mown, but a rank fawn mat criss-crossed

22

with the purple arching stems of brambles. Some of the grave-stones leaned crooked and many of their inscriptions were illegible; but slowly, as the tangle and decay grew worse, the jutting monuments became grander; at another crossway sat the first carved angel; ivy seethed around her knees and sent tentacles up to fondle her shoulders; she looked posed, intentional, as if the wilderness and ruin were proper to her. Beyond that the procession trudged through an area of mausoleums, wilder and more entangled still, though here and there some great-niece of the last deceased had kept the family tomb tended; pillars stood askew, gothic vaults had been patched with corrugated iron, buddleia seedlings sprouted from pediments. In places between these shanty-like monuments a fresh grave had been dug and filled and was marked with a modern headstone or a white wooden stake bearing only a number; the effect was like that of a Victorian suburb of large houses, plots of whose gardens are now sold as sites for neat new bungalows. At just such a site the cortege halted.

The undertaker's men hefted the coffin out. A train drummed past on the other side of the boundary wall, and by the time its noise faded the priest's ghastly mumble had begun.

Lydia was so withdrawn into herself, snail-like, against being touched by any of this dreary celebration that it took her some time to notice that four of the party had not come from Devon Crescent. Her attention was first caught by two men in short fawn coats who were acting in a non-mourning fashion, prancing and posing—who were in fact taking photographs. Lydia thought this excessive as an act of piety for a Government burying its charlady, until she saw that the photographers were aiming their cameras at two women on the far side of the grave, a tall pale girl also (to Lydia's relief) wearing trousers and a nondescript older woman in a dark blue coat. There was a touch of the old-fashioned nanny about this second woman, but the girl didn't look the type to have belonged to the nannied classes; her face was working, without tears, until she noticed the photographers and steadied herself. Then her features settled and she became Procne Newbury.

Lydia had never met Mrs Newbury's famous daughter, though she had been forced many times to look through the collection of press cuttings of the trial. Before that Mrs Newbury had often talked of herself as a sadly wronged mother, but when Procne had rocketed into notoriety she had been filled with pride and pleasure, as though it had been she who had lit the touch-paper. For Lydia this encounter by the graveside was like the thud of the stick falling.

As soon as the coffin had been lowered and the earth had rattled onto its lid Lydia slipped round the blind side of the crowd and walked straight up to Procne.

"Hello," she said. "I'm Lydia Timms. Your mother had a room in my house."

"Eff off," whispered Procne.

The nanny surged round from her far side.

"No talking to the prisoner, if you please," she said.

One tenet of Lydia's anti-authority creed was that underlings are victims too. She turned sympathetically to the warder.

"I thought Miss Newbury would like to hear about how her mother got on during the last few months," she said. "I saw quite a bit of her."

A policeman, hitherto unnoticed, loomed into the periphery of Lydia's vision.

"You can't do that here," said the warder. "If the prisoner wants a visit you'll have to arrange it through welfare."

At a nudge from her elbow Procne turned away and the two of them moved off towards a dark car which had been waiting further along the driveway. The policeman stayed where he was, watchful, as if suspecting the Livonian Government in Exile of being a cover organisation for a group bent on rescuing tarts from prison. One of the photographers blocked Lydia's view.

"I'd better have your name," he said. "They might want the one with you in it."

He had a trival beard and looked as though he hated mankind.

"Timms, L."

"Miss or Mrs?"

"Neither."

He was making an Oh-God face when Lydia heard a shout of "I'd like a visit, please, Miss." She stood clear and saw Procne climbing into the car. She waved to show she'd understood. Two more policemen emerged from behind tombs and climbed in also. Lydia smiled, thinking how thrilled Mrs Newbury would have been to know that her daughter had come to her funeral so grandly escorted.

"A very important prisoner," said Mr Vaklins at her elbow.

"Oh, I suppose there might have been a mob of sight-seers," said Lydia. "There are always people who will stand around for hours just to goggle at someone like that for a few minutes. Heavens, what wreaths! She'd have loved that."

They were hideous, piled in sheaves along the bank of artificial grass which covered the mound of sticky yellow clay from the grave. One or two seemed to be unconventional in shape, until Lydia realised that they were representations of the Viking horn which was the crest of the Livonian Republic. Now that the mummery was over Lydia almost smiled again—they seemed such absurdly appropriate ornaments for the tomb of an old battle-axe who had died drunk.

4

"You will give me to a hospital, won't you? Promise. None of this rubbish about the family vault. Honestly, I'd rather be turned into pet-food."

"I'll think about it, darling. Would you haunt me if I didn't? You'd make a very bad ghost—not your style at all."

"I'm serious."

"I know you are. When you're serious your voice drops and you speak very slowly, as though I'd suddenly gone soft in the head. But I can't take it seriously—I mean, if you think like you do, what does it matter what's done to you afterwards? The dead have a duty towards the living. Anyway, I want a great big marble slab on the wall of the church at Duxbury with eighteenth-century lettering—early eighteenth-century, please—enumerating my virtues and palliating my vices, and finishing with a bit of verse in Latin embodying a metaphysical conceit about . . ."

"Richard."

Beside her in the dark she felt the faint, almost Pavlonian response of tension in his muscles. She sighed to herself, remembering the time before his breakdown when they'd both merely thought it funny that that was his reaction to her use of his Christian name.

"It's all right," she said. "I'm not going to ask you to think about anything you don't want to. Just let's talk about something else. I shouldn't have started it."

"You don't think you ought to talk it out, if it's bothering you?"

"No. Listen, about Mrs N's room, have you any views?"

"What was she paying?"

"One pound fifty. She was controlled. I daresay I could have gone to the rent people and squeezed it up a bit, but I hadn't the heart. Now this Vaklins bloke wants it."

"Ask twelve."

"That's not the point. I mean, there's hundreds of people

who need it more than he does. If I could find some old biddy . . ."

"And ask one fifty?"

"No, she'd have to be able to afford four, somehow. I'd like her to come from somewhere round here, too."

"How much are they asking for the new flats at forty-six?"

"Forty for the basements, Mrs Tevell said, but that's not the point. They oughtn't to have been made into that sort of flat—it was monstrous. It was a typical Dice and Dottridge transaction."

"But they're estate agents. They aren't allowed to own property."

"Don't you believe it, darling. They're everywhere. They used a holding company. But don't you remember the Hoods who used to live there? That old man with the racing pigeons —his wife who used to scamper out with a carrot for the rag-and-bone man's horse?"

"Vaguely. They had a daughter in Canada."

"That's right. Dice and Dottridge gave them a silly little lump sum to move out and found them a high-rise flat in Acton. Mr Hood's dead. She's in a home."

"Poor old ducks. But the world's changing, Liz—you can't stop it."

"I *can*."

She slid her hand down his arm and twisted her fingers into his. She knew that he would let her do what she wanted, and wouldn't complain, even if it meant tap-water and scrag-end stews for months. So it was only fair to try to do things in a way which he too thought was reasonable.

"Suppose Mr Hood would have died anyway," she said, "and Mrs Hood gone into that home. Even so they must have had a time—eighteen months, two years—when they were completely miserable. If they'd been able to stay here, where they knew people . . ."

He squeezed her hand and chuckled.

"I love you," he said. "How are you going to phrase your ad for the new tenant? How are you going to screen the applicants for worthiness? Pay the rag-and-bone man to drive past and watch whether they reach for the carrots?"

Lydia was already worried about that. She hated the idea of using her power as a property-owner to discriminate between the needs of two or more people—it would be like

27

choosing a puppy in a pet-shop window.

"Suppose I don't let Mrs N's room at all," she said.

"Just keep it as a memorial to her?"

"No! Shut up! Listen. I get that beam out to-morrow. The dry-rot people come next week, and the damp-course people the week after. When they'd gone I was going to finish those rooms, move us in there and do these two. But suppose I simply get the beam back in—I've still got the floors to check, too—and then leave it and do Mrs N's room. I'll have to move the sink, but I can put a proper cooker in there if I don't tell the Council. Then I can persuade Mrs Pumice to move up. She's always behind with her rent because Don —Mr Pumice—is a swine about the maintenance, and if he's not here she doesn't need that extra room. Leave Doctor Ng where he is. The Pelletiers' tenancy runs out next month, and from one or two things she's said I know she's dead scared about what I'm going to ask for the new agreement, and with Stan married they don't need that little back room; so I think they'll be happy to go up into Mrs Pumice's and pay what they're paying now. That clears the first floor for the Evanses. I can put a bath and loo into Stan's old room, which'll mean they'll have their own bathroom and be all on one floor, and I know they won't mind paying a bit more for that. The men said the dry rot wasn't too bad in those two ground floor rooms, so we can move up to the ground floor . . ."

"We'll have it all to ourselves?"

"That's right. We'll need it. As soon as I've got the basement really nice and self-contained and bringing in some income I want to start having a baby."

"Oh . . . what sex?"

She rolled on her side to kick him, but either he misinterpreted her movement or his reactions were more dextrous than sometimes; at any rate the kick missed and his legs tangled round hers as his arm slid under her neck. The Timmses didn't make love one quarter as often as the sex-pundits say decent people should; Lydia liked it when things went right, but they didn't always, and quite often this was her fault. It wasn't that she resented her role, but she could never be sure when they began whether she was going to be able to melt herself into it. To-night, half-way through a first quite promising kiss, something fizzed inside her mind and spat out a gritty little thought; she knew it would be useless to go on until she'd said it aloud, so she eased her mouth free.

"It all depends on not finding any more horrors anywhere else," she said.

5

THE BIG BEAM in the back room, after a first few minutes of total obstinacy, came out with less trouble than Lydia had expected, as though it were tired of supporting the whole garden façade and were glad of a rest. Cataracts of fine mortar dust fell continuously along most of its length as Lydia levered it inchmeal onto the cradle of scaffolding she had built. The room smoked with the ancient, pinky-grey powder, but she'd known it would be like that so she was wearing a smog-mask over her nose and mouth. Four or five bricks came loose, making the beginnings of a ragged arch, but the Acrow hoists supported the ceiling so well that not a crack showed.

The beam must have weighed three hundredweight. At the tricky instant when it was balanced half on the brickwork and half on the cradle, a man coughed in the room behind her. No doubt he'd done it just to call attention to his presence, but once he'd started he was unable to stop; at each gasp his lungs sucked in fresh supplies of dust to aggravate the next spasm.

"Sorry," called Lydia, unable to look round. "I had to start without you. Why don't you wait in the passage till the dust clears. I'll be out in a couple of minutes."

But the man stayed where he was, gradually mastering his gullet once the beam was clear of the wall and ceased to drag out mortar as it came. The coughs diminished on a surprisingly deep note, like the retreating grumble of a thunderstorm. As soon as she was sure that the beam was firmly on the cradle Lydia turned.

He loomed through the dust-cloud, an enormous Indian in a linen suit, black shirt and yellow tie and turban. He was holding a bright pink handkerchief to his face.

"You are the man from the Council?" asked Lydia.

He grunted.

"I couldn't wait, you see," she said. "I wasn't sure that

you'd be coming at all, and I had to get on. It's quite safe, if you want to come and check. The joists above run north-and-south so the hoists take the weight there, and the wall really bears on the concrete lintel on the outside. Look, you can see clearly now."

He stepped prissily over and peered into the smoking cavity with bloodshot, bulbous eyes.

"All right?" said Lydia, suddenly anxious at his long silence.

"I know nothing about such matters," he said. "If it falls, that is God's will."

His eyes swivelled towards her, as if cueing her for the Amen. She could see the white all the way round each iris.

"I thought you said you were the man from the Council."

"I am the man from a Council. A man from the Council. Let's get out of here."

Lydia had already promised herself a cup of coffee as soon as she got the beam clear, so she led the way to the front room.

"You'll have to sit on the bed," she said as she put the kettle on. "We're living all in one room at the moment, while I get the rest of the basement sorted out. If you aren't from the Borough Council, who are you?"

She spoke sharply, because she resented this man who had materialised like a genie out of the smoke, first misleading her and then somehow taking charge of the situation, as if he had the right.

"I came to tell you about Bob Roberts. My name is Ambrose."

"Mine's Lydia," said Lydia, who approved strongly of instant first-name terms.

"Ah, in that case mine is Jack Ambrose. I will have hot milk, please. I must keep up my strength for my work."

Again Lydia had that sense of sleight-of-mind, as though he were deliberately strewing conclusions around for her to jump to. Despite the turban he didn't look or sound like an Indian. He had the feel of a ham actor, a heavy, one of those would-be giants of the stage who make up for their total lack of skill by imposing their own personality on the material. Mr Ambrose had a personality to impose, at least. She looked at him, full face. He looked back, unsmiling but bland. Powdered with the pale mortar-dust he might have been made of milk chocolate the whole way through. He wore several signet rings on each hand, like knuckle-dusters.

But there was plenty of milk, so she fetched it out of the fridge and put some in a saucepan.

"And who's Mr Roberts?" she said.

"A friend. You spoke to him about your garden."

"Oh, yes! I asked if he could come back to-morrow morning, but it was a bit vague, so I didn't really . . ."

"Of course. Bob is a good gardener. What is your proposal?"

"Well, I don't know how much time he's got. There isn't more to do here than would take a man one morning a week. But I know several of my neighbours would like a gardener too, so if he wanted more time than that . . ."

"Money?"

"The rate round here is eighty pence an hour, but if he's really a skilled gardener . . . I couldn't afford more than three pounds a week, in any case."

He didn't answer, but turned away and stood with his back to her, running his mailed fingers up and down the folds of his neck-muscles. The kettle screamed. Lydia switched off the gas, poured water on the coffee-powder, added a little cold milk and lifted the mug to her lips, only to find that she was still wearing her face-mask. This irritated her more than anything, because it was not like her to make such a mistake. It was Mr Ambrose's fault. He lay like an iron bar, thrown by hooligans across the smooth track of the morning. What's more, she damn near let his milk boil over too.

"Here you are," she snapped. "What's the problem? If he's a good gardener he can get twice that amount almost anywhere, so you needn't worry about turning me down."

"Ah, thank you for the milk," said Mr Ambrose, swinging round. "I will help myself to sugar, please. My strength, you know. The problem, Lydia, is our friend Bob. He has had, well, a certain amount of difficulty in recent years."

"Been inside, you mean," said Lydia. "I don't mind, provided it's not for molesting kids. I've got a small son. Otherwise I'd be glad to help."

"Ah, a social conscience," said Mr Ambrose, stirring his eighth spoonful of sugar into his milk. He sounded faintly mocking.

"Yes," said Lydia.

"Bob is a bit inadequate, it is true," said Mr Ambrose, after a pause. "He needs help and support. But he is honest, and a good gardener. That is all. He will be here on Monday morning at nine. I will leave it to you to make arrangements with your neighbours."

He sucked the scalding milk down in two gulps, smacked his lips and put the mug on the draining board.

"Eighty pence an hour, OK," he said. "Try to arrange five mornings a week. Bob will be here on Monday. Routine, routine. Good-bye. Thank you for the milk."

Huge though he was he seemed to glide away and had reached the door and gone before Lydia realised that the interview was over. She heard him climb the stairs, light-footed, three at a time.

She sat on the kitchen stool, becoming herself again, sipping slowly at her coffee and at first deliberately trying not to think about her own reactions to Mr Ambrose. This proved impossible, so as the coffee sank in the mug she settled down to organising her anger into parcels which she could cope with. Part of the problem was the shame of disliking a coloured man so strongly and instantly. Richard maintained that even in the most saintly and unprejudiced of mankind there is a sociological id, a demon of racial spite, which the sociological ego controls and represses. For the first time Lydia was afraid that he might be right. She asked herself whether, supposing he had been a white man but otherwise the same—as gross, as off-hand, as masterful—she would have treated him just the same. No—she would have counter-attacked, demanded to know what his interest was, refused him milk, even. (Milk? Why did she resent that so?)

But would she? Or would she have given in just as easily? Was her anger really no more than spite at being told what to do, having arrangements made for her, in her own house, by a man? Furthermore the man was somebody she ought in theory to approve of, helping the inadequate to find a place of comfort among the grinding cogs and trundling levers of the social system. Perhaps benevolence towards the underdog tends to balance out into insolence towards the comfortable, which the comfortable must tolerate and respect. A saint is entitled to his own bad breath, surely.

Coffee finished, Lydia rose with a sigh, tied her mask on again and went back to work. Most of the visible dust had settled, but minute particles still prickled in the air. She plugged in her inspection lamp and studied the beam, inch by inch. A little woodworm had attacked one corner, but she could find no trace of rot anywhere along it, nor in the cavity from which it came. All it needed was a good double dose of protective fluid and a blitz on the woodworm, and then it could simply go back. Thirty pounds saved! Three days gained!

She should have been singing, but as she cleaned up the dust, sprayed on the fluid and mixed a little cement to re-point the brickwork of the cavity, the ghost of Mr Ambrose seemed to stand behind her shoulder, ready to cough again.

6

THE BEAM CAME OUT on Thursday. Friday was spent getting it back and making good. Early on Saturday morning Richard sat up in bed, stretched and said "Let's go somewhere."

"If you make the arrangements," muttered Lydia, purring back into the nest of warmth in which she'd woken.

The week-end turned into an absurd little idyll, most of it spent plodding round a patch of Hampshire, among untarred lanes and across fields, while Richard and Dickie refought the Battle of Cheriton Wood from the strangely confused accounts of the Civil War diarists. It was brisk but not bitter weather, with a pale blue sky, snowdrops in the hedgerows, birds singing and hopping, pudgy lambs nuzzling at ewes' udders, and the noon sun strong enough to make summer seem quite near. The hired car didn't break down, the fisherman's inn on the Itchen contained no fishermen, and though it was fairly crowded with raucous near-gentry on Saturday night the Timmses went to bed early and treated the noise as though it had been sea-surge against cliffs under a hotel window. They lay talking for a long time, weary and fond, about nothing that concerns us.

7

THE SPY WAS RAPPING at the basement door when Lydia got back from taking Dickie to school. Approached from the other side, with the light full on him, he looked quite different, smaller, older—less, in fact, like a spy.

"You're Mr Roberts," said Lydia, running down the basement steps. "I'm sorry if I'm late."

"I don't know you're late," he said.

"Now, she said, "I've talked to some of my neighbours, and I think we can find you something to do every morning, Monday to Friday. We've all got the same lay-out, a bit of garden in front, mostly paved, and a bigger bit at the back. Mine's in an awful state, I'm afraid, because I don't like gardening and I've been throwing all sorts of building rubbish out and burning it. Come and have a look."

She led him through the basement and up into the litter and mire of the back garden. Mrs Pelletier was hanging her washing out. As usual, Mr Pelletier seemed to have got through twelve shirts in the week.

"I've tried to keep the rose-bed clear," said Lydia, "but the roses don't look very happy to me."

The spy shook his head, fingered a weary leaflet, poked his toe-cap into the slimy earth and grunted.

"I don't much care for roses anyway," said Lydia. "Look, I think the best thing, for a start, would be if I took you round to the other houses and introduced you. Then, if there's any time after that, you could make a start on my front garden. I don't think there's any point doing anything back here till I've finished the worst of my building."

"Best get that finished," he said.

Mrs Tevell was in, and garrulous. Mrs Schelling insisted on hobbling all round her domain, discussing every shrub. June Stoddart was having coffee and needed somebody to moan to about the loneliness and uselessness of wives. So it was nearly eleven when Lydia got home. That left her time before lunch to find the spy some tools, ring the prison to check that her visit to Procne was still in order, and give the back-room beam its final dosing of chemicals. It also meant that she had to pay the spy two pounds forty for an hour's work, but at least he had got a lot done in that hour—in fact it was extraordinary how spruce and lively the front garden now looked, with all the leaves and sweet-papers gone, and the wistaria pruned, and the black, winter-smeared soil raked and aerated. Despite the expense Lydia ate her lunch with a feeling of triumph at having made another step towards civilisation, and only a faint regret that Mr Roberts wasn't a spy. That really would have been using the system to beat the system. She was still a little worried by her inability to be certain whether he was the same man that she'd first met, but even if he wasn't that probably only meant that Mr Ambrose had sent along a different lame dog, a bloke who actually knew a buddleia from a buttercup. It would be typical of Mr Ambrose's dictatorial style not to tell her what he was doing.

Once upon a time, when criminals were still deported to Australia, they used to be kept waiting for shipment in the idiot squalor of the hulks. They were a suppuration, which eventually even our thick-skinned society noticed, and slapped a poultice on, and called it cured. Procne's prison had been part of the poultice, built on the south-eastern outskirts of London, not far from the main-line railway. Unfortunately the railway had attracted a suburb of fair-sized respectable houses, whose developers were distressed by the notion that house-buyers might wish to pay less for property so close to a prison, as though crime were a sort of marsh-fever that might seep out and infect the honest bourgeois. The balance was redressed by the prison architects, who made the prison look thoroughly, even grandly respectable—a close replica of the Château de Chambord, in fact. The gate-tower still looks stunning against the western sky as you walk up the dreary (and now quite unrespectable) avenue of Croydon Road.

Lydia hated the tower, and was not remotely interested in its history. Her clothes and skin seemed to melt into a hard, protective carapace as she waited at the gate for the warder to open to her knock; and waited again in the drab octagonal room where other visitors sat and smoked, all tense with the nearness of Authority; and waited finally in a pink, oppressive barrel-vaulted cell while a welfare officer went to fetch

37

Procne Newbury. The cell had been converted to an office, and contained a couple of chairs and a desk. Lists of names were Sellotaped to one wall and a Mucha poster of a dreamy pale woman, all gold, to another. There was a telephone and an overflowing ash-tray. But despite these signs of a live occupant, to Lydia it might have been an alcove in Richard's family vault. All that weight of sooty brick, all the weight of that other edifice whose bricks are warders and policemen and judges and Home Secretaries and respectable people, towered above her as a monstrous burial-mound. But Lydia didn't feel that she was buried as a body is buried. She was more like the bulb of a bluebell in a town garden over which paving-stones have been laid, but still the leaves find their way out to the light, heaving aside if necessary the crushing hundredweights of stone.

Outside little bell-like noises went to and fro as officers passed, all carrying their own bunch of keys. Lydia had brought cigarettes, knowing that that was expected; she herself smoked seldom, but she thought it would seem more natural, less Lady-Bountiful, if she already had an opened packet when Procne came, so she lit one and sucked the smoke in with shuddering relief. At last footsteps stopped at the cell door and keys jingled with a purpose. The Welfare Officer held the door open for Procne, who came rather hesitantly in.

"Will half an hour be enough?" asked the Welfare Officer, breezy and friendly but not waiting for an answer. The door closed and was locked. Lydia found that she was standing and smiling too, unnaturally, with a patch of tense muscle in either cheek. Procne looked back at her, cow-eyed, emotionless. They stayed like that for some time. Procne was six inches taller than Lydia; she wore her hair dyed silvery blonde, in a semi-afro frizz; except for her eyes her features were small, and her face was slightly flat, its skin very soft and coloured, partly with make-up and partly by nature, like a sentimental pastel of a child. A minute before all Lydia's thoughts and emotions had been a complex of angers and theories about the oppression-machine which surrounded her; now she was flooded with absurd longing and resentment, almost with jealousy. Procne's life was smashed, her future a foreseeable vista of shoddy notoriety and shoddy let-downs. Lydia's was still full of drive and promise and, even, love. But to be so beautiful! Impossible not to believe that it made everything else worth while.

38

"Wh-which chair would you like?" she said at last.

"I don't mind," said Procne in a dull voice.

They settled. Procne took a cigarette and lit it awkwardly. Slowly the strange mood seeped away.

"My name's Lydia—Lydia Timms. I came to tell you about your mother."

"I spose so. You butch?"

"No. At least I don't think so. I've never tried. Are you?" Procne shrugged.

"Sorry, what did you say your name was?" she said.

"Lydia. Or Liz."

"Lydia and Procne. Jesus, some parents want their heads looked at. Mine wasn't Mum's fault, not really. She wanted to call me Suez, but the parson wouldn't have it. She near as hit him, right there by the font, she told me. She was after something real unusual, see. Not some bleeding saint, neither. That's how they come to Procne. Dad always said it sounded like a bloody health-food."

"I never knew your father."

Procne nodded. She sat uncomfortably in her chair with the arm she wasn't using for smoking held stiffly across her stomach, as though in an invisible sling.

"But I got to know your mother pretty well these last few years," said Lydia. "I remember the first time I met her . . ."

It was a relief to be able to put into words what she had felt, but never till now formulated, about Mrs Newbury, what had made the old rogue, with her sharp-featured decisive head and slack, floppy, shambling body, so intricate, so amazing. There are some people, worthy and cultured, whose characters can be discussed and agreed on in five minutes; others will occupy a party of close friends all through a wet week-end, and Mrs Newbury was one of those. Quite soon Procne took her arm out of the imaginary sling, leaned forward, began to gesture agreement, and then started on her own store of childhood study. Mrs Newbury had been a houseful, a street of people, a world . . . Suddenly Lydia saw how proper it was that this estranged daughter should have wept so at her mother's funeral.

"Not that we got on, not really," Procne said. "She was always at me, never satisfied, trying to live my life, plans, plans, plans. My first bloke—not counting boys at school, acourse, I was only a kid then—he found me a lovely flat near Marble Arch, colour TV, the lot. Mum was ever so cross and snarky. Wasn't me setting up professional—he had to pay the rent somehow, didn't he?—but cos Mum hadn't found him for me herself. In the end it come so she'd just phone me up Thursdays and we'd have a long chat, and I didn't even go round, Christmas, with a present. She never come and visit me here, mind. Did she read all about my trial?"

"Oh yes—she kept a scrapbook. I'm afraid she rather revelled in it."

"Well, that's Mum—you can't hold it against her. In fact I'm glad she had her bit of fun. No fun for me, mind, shut away like this."

"I think it's absolutely disgraceful. All those time-serving hypocrites who'd have been queueing up to meet you if they'd had the chance, working out their stupid little repressions by smashing you to bits. I couldn't even read about it, I was so angry."

"D'you really think so, Liz? I know some judges what go with girls, but mine wasn't like that. I saw a picture of him in the papers with his family in front of his house. Two lovely daughters he had. Honest, I don't think he was like that."

"I didn't mean . . . oh, I'm sure you're right. I get a bit het up about the things we do to each other, sometimes. Your mother used to tell me . . ."

"How much rent she pay you?"

"One pound fifty. I hope it wasn't too much. It was what she was paying when we bought the house."

"Je-sus! You're another wants her head looked at! I always sent her ten quid a week to help with the rent."

Lydia laughed. It was so typical of Mrs Newbury—not that she'd ever had the feel of real poverty about her and had often said that old-age pensioners had nothing to grumble about and ought to be more grateful for what the Government did for them.

"Are you sure she got it?" she asked.

"All I know is that time I couldn't spare it . . ."

Suddenly Procne seemed to shrink back into the stolid, dull, institutionalized self she had been before they started talking about Mrs Newbury. She even glanced at the door, as if expecting to see an eye peering in through the peep-hole.

"What's the matter?" said Lydia.

Procne looked at her troubled.

"All right," she said, "I better tell you. I got to tell somebody, or I'll do my nut. You know I was saying about my bloke what found me that flat? Gavin's his name. We was doing OK, but he fancied himself as a businessman and he wanted to expand—get a few more girls on his books, all that. *I* didn't mind. Trouble was, he had big ideas but he didn't have the organisation, and after a bit he run into a mob what did. They done him proper—he's in Morocco, last I heard. It come at a bad time for me—I was due an abortion—it's not as nice as it says in the papers, really—so one thing and another the mob didn't realise at first I was—you know—valuable. So I was short, and Mum was getting at me, and I met this lordship at a party. He's quite famous but he's ever so forgetful, always leaving things in my flat, like, and sending his chauffeur round for them after. I just knew he wouldn't notice if I took a couple of his cheques, like, and he didn't. I wasn't greedy—just enough for Mum for a few weeks, and buy me a new trouser suit. Well, after that the mob cottoned on to what I was worth—it's funny, another lordship what works in the City told me it's just like that when one company does a take-over on another, they take a bit of time to sort out what they bought. Anyway the mob set me up proper again, and put in a bloke, Chris, to look after me and that, and I thought well this is a bit of OK. Chris is nice, and he can act posh, and he was too scared of the mob to beat me up the way Gavin sometimes done, but he was just like Gavin one way—he had ideas. When I told him about them cheques he said "We'll try a bit more of that." He worked it out that if we was careful whose cheques we borrowed— you know, blokes what wouldn't like to come out about their funny tastes, and that—we'd be OK. Only it didn't work out. We was ever so stupid, really. One thing, it was a mercy the police copped us before the mob found out. That would *not* have been funny."

Carried away by the vigour of her story-telling, Procne only came back in the last few words to remembering her fear of "the mob". Even then she only saw one part of the ugliness of it all, and didn't seem to realise that "the mob" was really only another section of the oppression-machine— the crudely stamped reverse of the medal whose obverse is Justice, elegantly engraved.

"They sound pretty frightening," said Lydia. "Could they really be spying on us here, though?"

"Not in here—we're off the wing. But I shouldn't be surprised they knew you was coming. I got a message from Chris. He's in Parkhurst, and first week he was there he had his face slashed and a couple of ribs broken. They'll leave him alone now . . . Cheer up, Liz, don't you worry—you'll never meet up with them."

"I hope not, but that isn't what bothers me. I hate being part of a society in which that sort of thing is allowed to exist."

"Nothing you can do about it, so why worry? What was we on about? Oh, yes, I was telling you about the cheques. Point is, Mum begun it."

"I don't think she realised."

"Course not, but she wouldn't of minded. Given her a kick, more like, thinking I done it for her sake. I wonder what she done with all that money."

"She may have spent it. She wasn't old enough to draw her pension, was she?"

"No, but there was Dad's from the railway, and what she was getting cleaning for them foreign gentlemen—she was ever so funny about them, sometimes. Used to tell me on the phone, all their little secrets—no, if she was only paying one fifty rent she wouldn't have no cause to spend what I was sending her."

"I don't know. Vodka costs getting on for . . ."

"Vodka! Mum never touched a drop! Never!"

"Oh. I didn't realise you didn't know. I'm so sorry. At the inquest . . ."

"You ever seen her drinking? Or drunk?

"As a matter of fact, no."

"There you are then. You can't keep it quiet, not in a lodging house like what you keep."

"We were all very surprised, but the evidence at the inquest semed clear. She was in pretty good condition, the pathologist said, but there was quite a lot of alcohol in her blood stream. She seemed to have been climbing up on her table to do something to her curtains, and she fell and hit her head on a brass fender. One of my other tenants, Mrs Pumice, went up next morning to ask your mother to mind her baby and found her lying there, still in the clothes she'd been wearing the night before. There was a bottle of Smirnoff on the mantelpiece and four empties in the cupboard. They all had her fingerprints on."

"Empties!"

"That's right."

"Never!"

"But . . ."

"Listen, Liz, when my Dad was drinking, the trouble Mum

42

went to to get the empties out of the house! She got a funny little basket on wheels and took the washing out to the public laundry in it, what she'd always used to do at home. She tucked the empties into the washing, see, and went to the laundry the long way round so as she could put the bottles into people's dustbins what wasn't her neighbours. Always."

"Even so, I suppose she might have been saving a batch up to get rid of. And . . ."

"Hey! You find out where she was buying the stuff?"

"I don't think the question came up. If you like I could . . ."

Procne, without asking, helped herself to another cigarette and lit it with shaking fingers. Her face seemed to have gone pale and textureless.

"Tisn't true," she said suddenly.

"I'm afraid it seems to be."

"No, it's only *evidence*. Evidence doesn't have to be true. I got sent down fair enough, seeing I done what they said I did. But you should of heard some of the evidence, both sides. I know. And I know Mum had a horror of drink, an absolute horror. My Dad was a bastard drunk—near as killed me when I was five. *I* drink. I've been to a party Friday night and next thing I know it's Tuesday and I don't know who I've been with or what I've done. That's what come between me and Mum, more than anything; she was always at me to pack it in, but it's my life, isn't it? Supposing she's been on the bottle, she'd have been a bit more friendly like, wouldn't she?"

"I don't know. Perhaps she only started drinking after you'd come here. We don't drink anything much at the moment because we haven't got any spare cash, so she didn't get at me. She did tell me about your father hurting you, and talked about the wickedness of drink in general—but you know, she did it with a sort of relish, slightly like a reformed drunk at a temperance meeting."

"Yes, that's Mum. It was all a play to her, wasn't it, with her acting all the best parts, too!"

Procne's laugh was surprisingly loud, but seemed to Lydia a completely natural sound, an expression of pure enjoyment of the instant, which the dreary hours coming before and after could never infect or alter. Most educated people have had a sheltered upbringing, because shelter makes the educator's task easier. Procne had not. For the past six years she had led a life which many people now-

43

adays would consider sophisticated, that is to say a life in close contact with violence, drama, risk and passion. You might have thought that by now she would be mature and knowledgeable, pickled in the brine of life. But she was naive, ignorant and unenquiring about the nature of the society that had used and crushed her. In fact she was not even aware that she had been crushed. Even here, in the heart of the burial mound, she fizzed like a child.

Lydia felt for her a strangely powerful flow of attraction and sympathy. In her own bustling life she had often fought with all her energy for odd underdogs and misfits; but these earlier episodes suddenly now seemed to her callow, sacrifices to her own conscience, Pharisaic in their rectitude and egoism. Procne was different. It seemed to Lydia of enormous importance, comparable almost to the love and protection she owed Richard and Dickie, that an area of freedom should be found in which Procne could live and expand and fulfil her enormous potential for happiness.

"All right," she said. "I'll tell you what I'll do. I'll try and find out where your mother was buying the drink. We ought to know. My father's a surgeon and knows a lot of medical people—I'll see if he can find out whether there was anything in the medical evidence that didn't come out at the inquest. And I'll try and find whether anyone knows anything about what she did with the money. I suppose that's the most important, because if there's any left it would be useful to have you come out."

"Ooh, yes," said Procne, evidently thinking of this point for the first time. "That would be ever so useful. Only, if she made a will. . ."

"I doubt it. She had a thing about lawyers. My husband is training to become a barrister, and she was always at me about it, suggesting other things he ought to do. She said lawyers were worse than criminals, all out to cheat you. I can't see her making a will."

"That's only Mum. Soon as she wanted a bloke she'd of gone and found one. One time, a bit after I set up with Gavin, she was on about making a will just to leave me out of it—course I only laughed. Never thought I'd need the money."

"OK, I'll see if I can find out about that too. She might have told Mrs Pumice."

"And the booze," said Procne earnestly. "Don't forget about the booze. That's screwy, Liz, I promise you. Any-

44

way, vodka! I mean, suppose she'd started drinking, it'd of been Scotch. Or gin. Can't you just see what she'd of said about vodka? Foreign muck! Don't know where it's been or what they've put in it! Dead men's feet! Sniff!"

Both voice and sniff were so accurate that the ghost of Mrs Newbury floated vividly through Lydia's mind and the hair on her nape prickled. They laughed together, and the conversation was still effortlessly flowing out of the suddenly opened spring of their friendship when the Welfare Officer came back.

"Thank you for coming," said Procne, rather formal in this new presence.

"I've loved it," said Lydia. "Thank you, too. Shall I see if they'll let me come again?"

"Ooh, would you? That'd be great!"

8

THE PATTERN, by which men came unnoticed into a room where Lydia was working, continued. They seldom offered to help, though.

"Can I help?" said a voice.

Lydia poked her head up between the joists. Mr Vaklins was standing by the door, wearing a dark mauve suit and an egg-yellow polo-necked jersey.

"You'd ruin that snappy get-up," she said.

"I have overalls in the car. What are you doing?"

"Just checking for dry rot under here. It's come in from next door, along that wall, and got into that cupboard. The question is how far it's spread. I've had that beam out and back, and it's OK, and so far I can't see anything under here, so we may be just in time. Did you come to ask about the room?"

"To see you and ask about the room."

"Oh . . . well . . . it's a bit difficult . . . I can't really make up my mind yet . . ."

"No hurry. I suppose the rent would be somewhere round twenty pounds a week?"

"Twenty! You could get somewhere much nicer for that!"

"Not a room in the same house as my work. You see, being a Minister is not a full-time job, so I would run my own business from here also. I've been using my flat as an office, and I've got used to sleeping above the shop, you know. You wouldn't mind if I put a telephone in?"

"Of course not," said Lydia, torn by the thought of the extra rent, and wine for Richard at supper, and a bike for Dickie, and a powder sander. "Hell . . . you see, the trouble is I've been sort of planning to use Mrs N's room to sort the tenancies out a bit. People have grown into this house all higgledy-piggledy, and now I think I could work it so that everybody lived on their own floor, with their own bathrooms and so on."

"Yes, I see . . . Are you going to have that wainscot off? Shall I do it?"

"You can't. Those sockets are live. Some nit seems to have done some private wiring, years ago, and as far as I can make out they come off the supply to the top two floors, so I can't switch them off without putting the Government out of action."

He shrugged, nodded and picked his way out.

It was almost pleasant to be back again in the dank, rank cavity beneath the joists; the problems here were at least inanimate (though sometimes it is hard to believe that the dry-rot fungus does not have a primitive, malevolent will of its own). Lit by the inspection-lamp the cavity was dreary but not gruesome; it smelt of town gas and mouse-droppings and the faint, sweetish, fallen-leaf reek of one of the wet-rots, whose brownish mycelium fanned out, pretty as sea-weed, along the party wall. The creak of footsteps came when Lydia was some distance away from her entrance-hole. By the time she had huddled her way back Mr Vaklins, in clean white overalls, was kneeling by the wall unscrewing one of the live sockets.

"Don't be a bloody fool," she snapped.

He turned, smiling, and spread out a hand which wore a heavy-duty rubber glove. Sulkily Lydia climbed out of the hole and stood by his shoulder, lighting his work with her inspection-lamp like a dutiful little woman, tense to cope if he made a mistake. He knew exactly what he was doing, though; his movements were quick, firm and deft. He'd brought his own little kit of electrical tools, which Lydia at once longed for in the way some women long for jewels; they seemed to her beautiful, neat and glistening in their wash-leather roll.

"Forgive me," he said, moving to the second socket. "I'm always inquisitive, especially about my hosts, the English. I don't quite understand why you're doing this—I mean doing it all yourself, crawling under floorboards, bashing away at plaster. I know some of your tenants only pay you a pit-tance, but the Livonians pay an economic rent, and your husband goes out to work. I'd have thought you could afford to hire men to do the worst of it."

Lydia approved of his asking so directly—it was what she would have done herself. That made her uncomfortable about having to hedge her answer; but Richard's breakdown was still no one's business but the Timmses'.

47

"Well," she said, "I do like to do things myself. That's partly because I enjoy it, and partly because it makes me feel a parasite if I buy someone else's time to do a job which I could perfectly well do myself. I mean, I'm not much good at plastering, so I'm happy to hire a plasterer—that's an art. But it makes me sick when I read—oh, there was a bloke in the *New Statesman* last year complaining in one breath about the exploitation of the working classes and the next that he couldn't find anyone to fix his slates at a reasonable price. *Anybody* can fix slates. But in fact you're wrong about Richard—he's not earning at the moment—he's studying law."

"Ah," said Mr Vaklins, apparently perfectly satisfied. But Lydia, having got that far, thought she owed both him and Richard more.

"He was a soldier when I married him. I hated the idea, but you know, one's in love, and besides his family had always been soldiers, and so on. I thought I could stick it out, but I couldn't. He did a stint as military attaché in a couple of places, but I couldn't even stand that. So he jacked it in."

"That must have been a wrench."

"Yes . . . well, we looked around and decided that he'd make a good lawyer. I wasn't going to have him doing some dreary job all day and then doing night school. Besides, he'd done it all for my sake, so now I thought it was up to me to support him. I didn't want to go out to work because of Dickie—that's our son—he's seven now. But my mother left me just enough money to buy this place—we got it cheap because of all the sitting tenants—and that's how I became a landlady. It suits me."

"It appears to, certainly. You wouldn't make a happy parasite."

His movements slowed. Rather thoughtfully he wrapped the last length of insulation tape round the earth wire, making a neat finish so that the end of the cable looked like the bandaged stub of an elfin limb. He rose slowly and gazed discontentedly at the results.

"I don't know if I shall stay in England," he said. "It is so full of parasites. Every society must have a few, I suppose, but in a way England has become like this house of yours, full of weak places and rots and moulds. Your tenants, my Government, we live here as though the house would go on just as before—and in England there isn't someone like you to repair the structure. They just slap on a bit of paint, blue or pink, over the worst bits. But you know, Lydia, when you've done you'll still have an old house, always in need of repair."

"You've got to do what you can," said Lydia.

"That is the rule?" (His voice sounded more foreign once he got away from small talk.)

"I don't know about rules. But if you let things go you never forgive yourself. Look, Paul, I haven't been quite honest about that room. It *would* suit me if I could get Mrs Pumice to move up there, and the rest of the tenants to sort themselves out. But . . . about parasites . . . I hate the idea of being one. I hate the idea of exploiting people just because my mother happened to leave me enough money to buy this house. I've never turned anyone out, and I keep the rents as low as I can, and even if all the tenants suddenly cleared out I wouldn't dream of converting to a lot of expensive flats for Biba people. I like tenants who have some sort of right to live here."

"Can we just rip this off, or must we be careful?"

"I'll get my crowbar."

As soon as she'd levered a gap big enough for him to get his fingers down he ripped the wainscot away as if it had been cardboard. Lydia crawled along with her inspection lamp. The fan of wet-rot had sent a tendril up this far but there seemed to be no sign at all of that faint, grey, cob-webby network which is the first wave of a dry-rot invasion.

"Great," she said. "It seems all clear. The damp-course men can do it the same time they do the front room. I'd been dreading what I'd find along here."

"What now?"

"Oh. Well, I've just got time to finish inspecting underneath before I go and fetch Dickie from school."

"May I take you? I'm at a loose end. Honestly."

She was about to refuse, out of a habit of independence, when she realised how enormously Dickie would enjoy a ride in that car. Carless, he longed for cars as petless children long for imagined furry friends.

"That would be marvellous," she said. "It gives me ten minutes extra, too. Can we leave at twelve fifteen?"

"I'll be there."

His smile and nod—even his stance—made it a relief for

49

her to slither into her musty catacomb and work off her embarrassment by scrabbling into dark nooks. The last conceivable thing she wanted was a dashing, rich, handsome, *helpful* admirer.

9

WITH BABIES Lydia let herself go. When she had been pregnant with Dickie, in Germany, she had read all the how-to-be-a-mother books she could find—in much the same spirit, Richard had said, as she'd have read all the manuals before deciding to buy a new car. She'd been alarmed by all the advice about a baby's need for fondling and for the stimulus and reassurance of touch, because she's felt this to be contrary to her own nature. So (again to Richard's amusement) she'd borrowed neighbouring babies to practise on, and had found that she had been wrong about her own nature, or perhaps about Nature. She had liked—loved—the touching and fondling.

Then Dickie had turned out an awkward baby, all elbows, and curiously cunning at folding a floppy little leg the wrong way; a wriggler, almost from the instant of birth. This might have been a factor inherited from either parent; or it might have been something to do with the insecurity caused by the slowly forming crisis that would take Richard out of the army; or even by the child perceiving before either parent the first signs of Richard's breakdown. Anyway, he'd never been fun to hold.

But Lydia still allowed herself to go soft with other people's babies; if challenged she'd have argued that it must be dangerous to suppress such a strong impulse in herself, but Mrs Pumice wasn't the type to raise questions like that. She was simply glad to have her baby held.

Trevor Pumice cannot have been the Health Visitor's delight; his skin had a yellowish tinge and he was about two pounds overweight. He was still very bald at an age when Dickie had sprouted a handsome thatch. Though not yet teething he dribbled. But he fitted his head into the hollow by Lydia's collar-bone, allowed one gross little hand to slide across the fullness of her breast and fell instantly asleep.

Mrs Pumice, also yellow-skinned and overweight, smiled

and lit a fresh cigarette from the stub of her old one. She had had her seventeenth birthday a week after Trevor was born.

"Crying half the night again," she said. "Now he'll sleep all day and wake up in time to cry all night."

"Poor you," said Lydia. "Dickie was hell at that age, too. It's the most tiring thing in the world."

"It's not being tired I mind, only it's so dead boring. But I'm glad you come. I was meaning to ask, will it be all right about the rent for a few days?"

"Is Mr Pumice out of work again?"

"I don't think so. I haven't heard nothing, and I expect I'd of heard if it was that. You see, it'd be a bit of an excuse for him getting so far behind with my payments, wouldn't it?"

"Oh dear. I suppose it's all right, Mrs Pumice. I won't turn you out, or anything, I mean. But I really can't afford to let you get tremendously behind. Look, I'm going to put a proper cooker into Mrs Newbury's room, and paint and paper it. When that's done, I wonder whether you'd like to move up there; it's less than half the rent, and you can have the pick of the furniture out of both sets of rooms, if you want."

Mrs Pumice's round, spiritless face went blanker still, but the look in her pale brown eyes hardened. Lydia didn't resent this—it was natural that somebody already so cheated by life as Mrs Pumice should regard any proposal at all as the start of yet another confidence trick. She gave her time to think by wiping away Trevor's steady, frothy dribble. The baby stirred, stretched and snuggled back. Lydia smiled at him.

"I'm going to have another of my own as soon as I can get a bit more sorted out," she said.

"That what you want me to move up to Ma Newbury's for?"

(Mrs Newbury, after her break with Procne, had tended to treat Mrs Pumice as a surrogate daughter. Mrs Pumice had resented this but had also in a way welcomed it, as even resentment was better than nothing at all in the vacuum of her life.)

"Not really," said Lydia. "I simply want to sort things out."

She explained carefully just how. Mrs Pumice's frown deepened.

"But what'll I do when Don comes back?" she burst out, clearly not having listened to half of what Lydia was saying. Don's return was a piece of future myth, in the sense that the arrival of Apollo at Delphi is a piece of past myth, and of much the same order of credibility. It was safe to promise almost anything against that event.

"With luck I'll have the basement ready by then," said Lydia.

"Oooh, well . . ." (Another thought slowly penetrated.) "If I'm saving that lot of rent I could trade in my TV for colour."

Lydia achieved a smile. Mrs. Pumice already smoked the rent she'd be saving, plus the rent she owed. This was no moment to start the old argument about having part of Don's wages attached; Mrs Pumice simply said you couldn't expect a man to put up with that kind of treatment. It was better to move the conversation elsewhere.

"Did Mrs Newbury give you any papers to look after?" Lydia asked.

"Not really," said Mrs Pumice, still thinking about colour TV.

"You see, I was talking to her daughter last week . . ."

"Were you? Honest?"

In a flash the whole atmosphere changed. The dreary room seemed to withdraw its weight of boredom as Mrs Pumice leaned forward, greedy-eyed. A tinge of health glowed in her cheeks. Her lips, half open, glistened.

"Yes, I went to explain about her mother's death."

"In prison!"

"That's right. I liked her. I think she's been very unfairly treated."

"Brought it on herself, Ma Newbury said. Ruined by drink, she said."

"That reminds me—did you have any idea that Mrs Newbury was drinking so much herself?"

"Cunning old bitch—you could of knocked me down with a feather. But what about Procne?"

"Oh . . . I told her I'd find out whether her mother had left her anything, or made a will. I thought perhaps you . . ."

"She was *making* a will. I mean, she was on about me not being able to sign it, cos I was under eighteen. I never seen it. Nothing to leave, had she? Drunk it all."

"I don't know. I just said I'd find out. When was this?"

"Ooh . . . bit before Christmas. She was on about how

53

ungrateful Procne was, and what a nice lady Princess Anne was. I don't know as she actually got it written out proper, but if she did I bet she got it signed all right. She might of burnt it after, perhaps, so as she could get a thrill out of being that noble and forgiving . . ."

It was a measure of the vigour of Mrs Newbury's personality, her heroic scale, that even the totally self-absorbed Mrs Pumice was able to sketch a vivid outline of how she might have behaved.

"I don't suppose there's much point in searching her room," said Lydia. "The police must have done that."

"Him!" said Mrs Pumice. "Down here for cuppas half the time, on about what a hard life it was. But Procne . . . She OK? How's she doing her hair now? What's it like in there?"

"Inside? It's exactly my idea of hell. It's a system designed to grind you down."

Lydia was about to expand on the society-induced apathy and loneliness of prison life when she saw that it wouldn't seem much different from the life Mrs Pumice herself lived. So she notched up a resolution to find excuses for visiting her tenant more often and switched to a description of Procne's coiffure.

"She really is beautiful," she added. "The photographs don't give you any idea."

"Oh, I seen her."

"I thought she'd never come here."

"No, Ma Newbury got it into her head to go to court one day and drug me along. I seen her then."

"She didn't tell me."

"Well, she loved a bit of a secret, didn't she? Fact, she made me promise not to tell. But then, being her, she got talking with some bloke and the next thing I knew we was in the papers. Look, I nicked the picture out of her collection —something to show Don when he comes back, see?"

She lumbered out of her chair and fetched from a collection of papers jammed behind a biscuit tin a clipping from the *Sun*, already yellow and brittle. Mrs Pumice, in the left foreground, might have been any bun-faced gawper. Mrs Newbury, in the centre, was herself even to the exact angle of her snapping-turtle head as it poked from her awful fur tippet. Over to the right, a bit further off, stood a very large, solemn Indian. It took Lydia a while even to notice him, and a while more to realise that he was Mr Jack Ambrose.

She was startled until she saw that the coincidence wasn't

54

all that strange. A man whose job is to help the inadequate must quite often find himself hanging around the courts. Still, the sight of him there, and the tenuous connection to Procne, depressed her. But what mattered was the good likeness of Mrs Newbury.

"May I borrow this for a couple of days?" she said. "I'll let you have it back."

"OK," said Mrs Pumice, wholly uninquisitive. "My, Trev fancies you, don't he? You wouldn't like to keep him?"

Her joky tone only half hid the wistfulness behind the question. Lydia was not conscious of any movement in herself, but the baby seemed to sense her inner rejection, waking into a whine. Carefully she petted him back to oblivion.

"I fancy him too," she said. "I'd love to look after him sometimes if you want to get out."

"Would you really? That'd be great!"

Those were exactly the words Procne had used, in the heart of *her* prison. Lydia was shocked at the difference in her own reactions—her eagerness to go back to Holloway, her grudging acceptance of a duty to take Trevor over and let Mrs Pumice escape for a few hours.

"Yes, I'd love to," said said. "Any time."

10

"I'M A BIT DRUNK," said Richard, drowsily. "One bottle of plonk, only. What was that in aid of?"

"I can explain everything," wheedled Lydia.

"The trouble is we've got out of the habit. Do you remember that restaurant in Salzburg where we knocked back four bottles after *Rosenkavelier?* I can't remember much about the opera, but the hangover remains vivid. You don't suffer at all."

"You drank twice as much as I did. One of the things I really like about the way we live now is not having to go to any more operas."

"I've got twice your mass, so I ought to be able to absorb twice as much alcohol. What was it in aid of to-night? Celebration of moving in here?"

"Not really—at least I hadn't thought of that. It's funny about fresh plaster. It's got a sort of white smell, even in the dark."

"Hyperaesthesia, they call it. Where do you strike next?"

"Mrs Newbury's. I'm pretty sure Mrs Pumice will move up, and that means Paul can't have it."

"I thought you like him."

"I do. When he's serious, and when he's doing things. But . . . anyway, whether I like him doesn't matter."

"Umm. What was the wine in aid of, then?"

"Nothing. I just felt I had to buy it because the bloke in the off licence was so helpful. It's that one at the bottom of Addison Avenue."

"Aren't there some nearer than that? At least four, I make it. Helpful about what, anyway?"

"Oh, recognising Mrs Newbury. Mrs Pumice lent me a photo of her. The bloke said she went there every week to pick up an order. You remember her old red shopping bag with the black rim? It turns out she had two of those, and she'd take one of them back every Tuesday morning, full of empties, and he'd have the other one ready and hand it over —six bottles of vodka and one of brandy. She gave him the money and took the change and went. She never said a word. He told me he'd inherited the system from the bloke who was there before him, and he didn't even know her name. If there was someone in the shop she'd walk past and come back when it was empty. He didn't even know she was dead. He'd still got the last order waiting—he showed me. And he never asked why I wanted to know, or anything, so I felt I had to buy something. I liked it, actually."

"So did I. When I'm a judge we'll have a couple every night, unless we're going to the opera. What does vodka cost?"

"Three oh nine. I looked."

"Plus the brandy. Over twenty quid a week. Where the hell was she getting it from?"

"Well, Procne was sending her ten quid a week. Richard?"

He tensed at his name, but only a little. Perhaps the wine helped. For a moment Lydia wondered whether that had been her subconscious motive in buying it.

"Ung?" he said, wary.

"What's going to happen to Procne?"

"The *News of the World* will pay two thousand quid for her life story in six instalments. There might be another thousand from a book. After that, if she's got any sense she'll emigrate."

"Don't be a bloody man of the world. What will *happen* to her?"

"Sorry . . . I hadn't got it that you minded . . . wheeee! You want her to come here?"

"What do you think?"

"Provided she doesn't bring her work home . . . damn! Sorry. That's the wine. What do I think? My first thought is you're nuts—only I know you're not. So . . . ummmm . . ."

"You see, darling, I've read again and again that when you come out of jail or a mental home or something like that . . ."

"The army . . ."

"Shut up or I'll bite you. The point is you've got to have something to do, somewhere to live, and a community to live in which accepts and supports you. Otherwise you simply go back and do whatever you did again. I think I'm probably the only person she knows who doesn't belong to her old world. I mean, if she wants to go back there, that's her decision. But we could at least offer her a choice. I think we ought to. Darling?"

"Ung . . . if you put it like that . . . I don't know . . . all the empties were vodka? No brandy?"

Richard's technique for not thinking about what bothered him was to think about something else. He did it quite deliberately. Sometimes Lydia had woken in the small hours to hear him murmuring lists of names—every man who had served in some company with him, all the cricket teams at his prep school.

"She'd probably dumped those," she said.

"You went to her room quite a bit, didn't you?"

"Why?"

"Vodka doesn't smell. Brandy does. Besides, six bottles a week of hard liquor—even Jack Arbuthnott didn't quite reach that level. Where the hell was she getting twenty-five quid a week? Six quid from the Government, say six from her pension, ten from Procne . . . you know, that ten from Procne sounds a little bit like blackmail. Perhaps there was someone else."

"Only too likely," sighed Lydia. "She had a Mafia outlook on life. Or she might have been nicking the Government's stamp money. She was awful. I miss her."

"Umm . . . suppose you decided to let Procne come, you could say to this Vaklins chap that he could have the room till then. Honestly, Liz, you could do with the cash."

"I know. But I really do want to take the chance to move the tenants into more sensible rooms. Besides . . ."

"Does he bother you? Am I going to have to unpack my hunting whip? I wonder where the hell it is."

"Yes, he bothers me, but not like that. I mean, at first I thought it was like that, you know the 'I'm a man and you're a woman so it's my nature to admire and court you and your nature to pretend not to like it but eventually succumb with gladness' bit. But I think that's only a manner, a sort of foreign politeness. There's something else—I don't quite know what."

Richard chuckled in the dark and squeezed her hand.

"Just a bit too eager to please," he said. "Perhaps if you gave him the room he might slack off a bit."

"I don't know."

"Or you could find him an outside interest."

"I'm sure he's got plenty. He really is very handsome in

58

a slightly gnomish way. I get an occasional urge to scribble a moustache on his face."

"Umm. What's Lalage up to?"

"Last I heard she's walked out of her job. I don't keep up with her love life."

"It's worth a try. Let's have a beano. I'm beginning to feel a bit hermit-like."

"I'll ask her when I see her."

"Great. That's fixed."

After that the conversation became spasmodic. Between whiles Lydia cast up mental minutes of the meeting. It had been agreed that if when the upheavals were over a room became available Paul should be offered it until Procne needed it, but that Procne could come if she wanted to. But as Richard had given more than Lydia to reach this compromise, she'd compensate by setting up a proper dinner party for him, with the family silver gleaming in the candle-light and all the other bloody trimmings.

11

IT WAS JUST BAD LUCK that the day Lydia wanted to start on Mrs Newbury's room was Dickie's half term. She was planning bus-routes for a round trip taking in The Army Museum, the Imperial War Museum, Apsley House and the Armoury at the Tower when Mrs Pumice knocked at the door and came in without waiting for an answer. She was wearing flared orange trousers, a purple jersey and a cap to match the trousers. Her baby whined on her arm.

"Oh, I'm ever so sorry," she said. "I got to go out. It's ever so urgent. I was hoping you could look after Trev for a couple of hours. He's got a bit of a grizzle, like, but you're ever so good with him."

It was the first time she had asked. It was impossible to refuse. So Lydia smiled and took the child; with minimal thanks Mrs Pumice was gone, eager and excited, as if she were dashing to meet a lover who was waiting for her somewhere in the snapping February wind.

"It isn't fair," said Dickie. "It's my half term."

"I'm sorry darling. I'll just see if I can get him to sleep, then we can go and throw furniture about in Mrs Newbury's room. We might even find treasure."

Trevor refused to sleep. His whine wasn't anything burpable, and didn't seem to be a teething noise, it was just an expression of generalised vague discontent, much like his mother's normal view of the world. Dickie tried to interest him in being a besieged army in a fortress of furniture, but that didn't work either. In the end Lydia humped him, still whining, up to Mrs Pumice's room, where she changed him and dumped him in a carricot. This she carried up the next flight and deposited on the landing outside the Government's front door, as though he were a bastard they'd jointly fathered. Dickie fought a heroic retreat up the stairs behind her, dying gloriously three times on the way.

"OK," said Lydia, "we'll start by looking for treasure."

Dickie enjoyed that. He rooted unsystematically among the drawers, hurling around Mrs Newbury's incredible musty old garments, until he came across a huge whale-boned cor- set which he decided could be worn upside down as a breast- plate. Strapped into this he held the bed against an attacking army while Lydia put the clothes back and searched any- where he hadn't rifled. There was no sign of money or will. Outside the door Trevor's whine at last stilled into sleep.

"Now, darling," said Lydia, "the next thing is to get all the furniture over here. Then we can roll the carpet up. Do you want a ride?"

The bed became a tank. A brief engagement with a panzer division was fought. Lydia was practised in using her slight weight efficiently, but she'd forgotten how Mrs Newbury had managed to accumulate all the heaviest furniture in the house. In particular there was a vast satinwood wardrobe against the inner wall, which could wait for the moment but would have to come to pieces before she could shift it. While Dickie bounced untiring on the bed she hoicked the tacks out of the carpet and began to roll it up, away from the window. As she worked she became vaguely conscious of a smell—not gas, not Mrs Newbury (who had generated her own strong odour of tea and shampoo and chocolate bis- cuits), not that reek of age and poverty which had filled the house when she'd first bought it, none of the rots she knew. She had a moment of sick despair about the rots, until she realised that what she was remembering was not the odour of any fungus but of the solvent that carried the fungicides.

When she'd rolled the carpet a few feet she slipped tup- pence under the far end, then rose and walked round the room, sniffing. The strange smell seemed strongest in the corner by the wardrobe.

"Are you smelling for treasure?" said Dickie.

"I don't know. Come here and see what you think."

At once he was on hands and knees beside her, sniffing like a snuff-addict, rump taut.

"Dead man's chest," he said in a puzzled voice.

(One of Richard's family traditions was that children with colds must have their chests rubbed with Vick. During the process the adult who was rubbing had to sing the pirates' catch from *Treasure Island*. This mightn't help the child to get better, but it was the Right Thing to Do.)

"Yes, it does smell a bit like that," said Lydia. "It seems stronger higher up. Oh, look!"

The satin in the corner of the ceiling was not very noticeable, but Lydia was reasonably sure it was new. She pulled the table over, stood on it and reached up. The patch was sticky to the touch, and whatever it was had dribbled a little way down the corner where the walls met; the smell on her fingertips was resinous but not really chemical. Could even a weeping fungus weep such tears? As far as she could remember the room directly above was the one in which the Government filed their documents, chiefly evidence for claims for compensation against Soviet Russia when freedom and democracy once again dawned in Livonia.

She would have liked to go and investigate, but could hardly walk in on the Government with Trevor whining on her shoulder and Dickie winkling out machine-gun nests behind her.

"Come and help me with the carpet, darling," she said. "It's getting a bit heavy for me alone. You push at that end."

Dickie got down and heaved against the roll with such verve that it trundled forward all askew and he tumbled after it, missing the planted tuppence. Still he was thrilled when Lydia pointed it out and went back to the bed to bounce, holding it high over his head and whooping at each bounce. Outside on the landing the baby joined in. The door opened.

"Sorry," said Paul Vaklins. "I've woken someone's child. Can I help?"

"I can manage, except for that wardrobe," said Lydia. "It comes to bits. I'd like to get it over there. Oh, damn that bloody kid!"

"Me?" asked Dickie, very interested.

"Of course not, darling. Sorry, Paul. Look, that sort of cornice thing lifts off . . ."

The wardrobe was like a vast Chinese puzzle, separate shapes self-locked to each other. The cornice was light enough, but the first section of actual hanging-space seemed to weigh several hundredweight.

"Whew!" said Lydia, as they settled it down by the window. "Thanks. I couldn't have done that alone."

"I'm glad to hear it. You sometimes give the impression that you can do anything. Hello!"

Paul had strolled back to where the other half of the wardrobe stood, tall but proportionless, displaying a cobwebby interface. The end section of the pedestal had fallen out sideways. Paul bent and picked up a large brown envelope, to which a smaller white envelope had been taped.

"It appears to be for you," he said in an amused voice.

"Treasure!" shouted Dickie.

"Family letters or something, I should think," said Lydia dryly. "Drat that kid, I'll have to go and change him. Let's get this other bit across, then I can manage."

"Can I open the treasure?" asked Dickie.

"No, darling," said Lydia. Her hand shook as she took the envelope from Paul and put it on the mantelpiece. As they hefted the other half of the wardrobe across she collected her wits. The feel of the envelope had certainly been that it held banknotes; there was no reason to be panicky and secretive; all she need feel was excitement at Procne's good fortune. On the other hand, there was no sense in telling the world.

"I must cope with that poor child," she said as she carried the pedestal across. "Dickie, will you be all right here for a bit?"

"I want to see the treasure," said Dickie.

"You stay here with me and I'll tell you a story," said Paul.

"A battle?" asked Dickie.

"There used to be some pretty scary witches in Livonia."

"A battle," said Dickie. "I'll make the sand table. Here."

He jumped off the bed and hoicked its cover into a range of mountains.

"I'm sorry," said Lydia. "His grandfather is a nut on military history. You don't have to do it, honestly, Paul."

"No, that's fine," said Paul. "I was in a sort of battle once. I'll tell you how Aaku Aakisen ambushed the Russian slave-train and rescued the prisoners. OK?

"That's marvellous," said Lydia. "You don't know what you've let yourself in for, though. I'll be about five minutes."

She snatched the envelope off the mantelpiece, ran out and whisked the carricot down the stairs with such acceleration that Trevor was startled out of his whine. She grabbed the pot out of Mrs Pumice's room, rushed him down to the basement and plonked him down on it. His whine modulated into a wail, but she ignored him.

The money was in five-pound notes, in labelled bundles of £200. There were five of these and a thinner one containing £165. Just under twelve hundred quid. The envelope contained one piece of lined writing-paper covered with Mrs Newbury's large and spiky script. It said:

I, Doris Newbury, of 11 Devon Crescent, London W.11, being in my right mind and all that, undo all my

63

other wills, not that I have made any as I remember, and leave this money and everything else I got to Lydia Timms, Lady Timms that is, for her boy Dickie to have when he grows up, and I do NOT leave anything to my own daughter Procne, that's been a pain in the neck to me no matter how I've tried. Signed by me Doris Newbury on the 12th of Jan, being in my right mind like I said.

She had signed with vigour, but had not asked anyone to witness the will.

Lydia read it again, sighing.

"Silly old bitch," she said, out loud.

She held the paper over her sink to burn it. Trevor stopped whining to stare in astonishment at the creeping flame, vivid in the gloom of the basement. When the paper was ashes Lydia broke them up smaller, turned on the cold tap and eased them down the drain. As she carried Trevor, clean and dry but still grizzling, back up the stairs, her shoulder bag containing twelve hundred pounds bounced menacingly against her other hip.

"Slowly the slave-train stopped," Paul was saying. "Wheeee, ssshhhh."

"Tonkatonkatonkatonktonktonk," added Dickie, always the perfectionist where stage effects were concerned.

Three pens tied with thread lay end to end in a valley on the white bedcover. The valley was blocked by a tumbled heap of paper pellets. Paul and Dickie craned over the scene, like the Gods above Troy.

"Now," said Paul, "old Aaku wanted the Russians to think that the avalanche was an accident until all the guards were out of the train and he'd blocked the line behind—otherwise they'd just reverse out. From the hillside he watched the soldiers climb out. Their uniforms looked black against the snow ..."

Lydia crept out and rang the bell of the Government's inner door. After a long wait Mr Obb opened it. He smiled with pleasure when he saw her, then stared doubtfully at the baby. The baby stopped whining and stared back. Their faces had a lot in common, blankness, baldness and an innocent bleariness of eye.

"I'm sorry to bother you," said Lydia. "I've just started to redecorate Mrs Newbury's room, and I've found a place

64

where something has leaked down from above. I don't know whether it comes from outside or from that room where you keep your files. Can I come and look?"

Mr Obb shrugged. For a moment Lydia thought he was going to refuse, but he smiled again and held the door open. Trevor, on being taken into an unfamiliar part of the house, snuggled closer against her side but stayed silent, as though instinctively aware of protocol. The filing room was a fair size, the same as Mrs Newbury's but with a lower ceiling and smaller window. It was so crammed with filing cabinets that it seemed claustrophobic. A narrow alleyway led straight from the door between two ranks of cabinets, all at least five feet high and piled on top with bundles of documents, completely screening the corner where the leak had come through. At the end of this alley Lydia found another rank of cabinets backed onto the one she had just passed, and another faced that, and another backed onto that, facing the far wall. But here there was a change—instead of a final rank lining the wall she found four large barrels and two big plastic dustbins. Until she had almost reached them the dusty dry odour of old documents had obscured this other smell, but now it was unmistakably the same as that of the leak below. She stood and stared, petting the baby absent-mindedly.

"What on earth . . ." she began.

"Oh, oh," said Mr Obb in a worried voice, "I had not thought. Of course, of course, Yes."

"I don't get it."

"This is where we make our *varosh*—our vodka."

"You aren't running a still, for heaven's sake?"

"Still? Ah, distillation. No, no, no. We, tsk, tsk, tsk, infuse, yes?"

"Are all these things full, Mr Obb?"

As she reached her free hand towards the lid of the nearer bin Mr Obb seized her elbow, squeaking with alarm.

"No, no, no! Not to touch, please! *Varosh* is most infectable!"

"I'm sorry," said Lydia, withdrawing. "I was worried about the weight. I hadn't realised how much you kept in here. I don't know whether the joists will stand it. This is an old house, you know."

Mr Obb stood back, stroking his bald head and looking vaguely relieved, as though the collapse of the floor were a

65

minor problem compared with the invasion of his booze by some bug.

"We have kept all these things here for many years," he said.

"Well, let's hope it's OK. I'll ring up the Building Centre and see whether they have any standards for the strength of floors supporting filing cabinets. You've got rows—eight in a row, forty. What about the barrels?"

"Oh, ah. Linden would know. Yes. Two barrels and one bin are always full. Sometimes the third barrel."

Lydia measured them with her eye. About forty gallons in the barrels and twenty in the bins. If it had been water, that would make a bit over half a ton. Say a couple of hundredweight each for the cabinets. Another four tons. Say five in all, minimum. It ought to be just about OK, provided the joists were sound. She nodded.

"OK," she said. "Now, do you know how much got spilt? I've got to have some idea how long it's going to keep coming through."

Mr Obb made vague gestures with his hands, a poor method of indicating liquid volume.

"Perhaps two litres, perhaps three," he said at last. "We had an old man, a servant, who made excellent *varosh*, very skilled, very careful. But then he died..."

"In this house?"

"No, no," said Mr Obb, suddenly vehement again. "*Not* in this house. But... yes, Count Linden and I were changing the liquor from one stage to the next when Linden dropped the jug. It is a fault of education. To be not clever with one's hands is a mark of the intellectual—in Linden's case of the aristocrat, of course. How could old Linden have known that the day would come when his heir must make his own *varosh*? Tsk, tsk."

It was impossible to dislike Mr Obb, even when he burbled class-ridden nonsense like this. In fact he seemed naively eager to placate Lydia's wrath at the spillage, as ingratiating as a savage who has committed some venial murder and is trying to explain his harmlessness and goodwill to a District Officer—a comparison out of another world which no longer exists and so can now also have its iniquities smiled at. Mr Obb mimed shame, and eagerness to please, and promises that he and Count Linden would never again throw sticky liquors around. Trevor Pumice gazed at him with a look of mild distrust.

"I expect it will be all right," said Lydia. "If it keeps coming through I can line that bit with foil before I paper."

"We will pay, of course."

It's hard to guess why Lydia's mind, occupied by the practical problem of stopping strong drink from penetrating a fresh-painted ceiling, should have at that moment made a lateral leap.

"You top the bins up with vodka and brandy," she said. "Mrs Newbury used to buy it for you."

"Yes, yes," agreed Mr Obb. "You see, we are spied on, all of the time. We must be most careful to do nothing that will make bad propaganda. We must not allow the Muscovites to say in Livonia that we spend government income on *varosh*. We do not, of course. We spend our own money."

Lydia would have like to ask for more details, but was afraid that if she did so he would put two and two together and find out that Mrs Newbury had been cheating them. As soon as she took a step away from the barrels he scuttered to the door and held it open for her. Down the corridor she could hear General Busch's rasping voice, speaking German behind a closed door.

"Political matters," said Mr Obb, relaxing. "A man from *Der Spiegel* is interviewing Busch about the death of Aakisen. The tragedy has created great interest on the continent."

"Heavens!" said Lydia. "I must rush. Poor Paul Vaklins is still telling Dickie about how Aakisen stopped the slave-train."

"Not Aakisen," said Mr Obb. "That was an episode in the Estonian resistance—a good story, however. Quite true."

"Let's hope Dickie doesn't find out. He disapproves strongly of fiction—it's his grandfather's fault. I'll let you know whether the Building Centre people think that floor's safe. Oh, can you remember exactly when you spilt the stuff?"

"Indeed," said Mr Obb. "It was the night before the funeral. Linden was tired with his vigil by the coffin—that is how he dropped the jug."

"Thanks," said Lydia. "I'll let myself out. Sorry to have bothered you."

"Delighted, delighted," said Mr Obb, his relief at getting rid of her so obvious that Lydia ran down the stairs wondering what on earth the old men were up to that they were so anxious to hide. Probably some piece of Baltic politics, so mummified that it no longer mattered to anybody except themselves.

A Mig howled over Mrs Newbury's bed. Paul did the jet-scream and Dickie the guns.

"Wheeeeeeeeeeeee."

"Tack attack attack attack attack tack."

It curved away over a coarsely darned hill-ridge.

"The prisoners ran between the pine trees," said Paul. "The bullets made lines across the snow like the tracks of a running deer. They threw white splinters from the pine-trunks. Women screamed. A man carried his dead son up the hill, but the bullets caught him and he himself fell dead across the body. The smoke from the wrecked train was like a war-signal, calling to the Russian garrisons. The prisoners wanted to scatter, to hide, to crouch down in the snow, to go back and surrender. But Aaku was their sheepdog, old Aaku with his sticky-out ears. He kept them fleeing in one bunch, all up the hill where the trees were thickest. Fresh groups of his men waited to help the prisoners and to pin down the pursuit. See, now, here is the hill-crest, where the sledges were waiting, and rough little ponies. They pile the women and the wounded on and race down the far slope. Night comes soon in our winters. It is dusk when they reach the frozen river. All along the ice the explosives are set. They cross, and . . ."

His fingers made explosions on the dust sheet.

"Boom! Boom! Boom!" yelled Dickie.

"So now the river was a defence line, and beyond it lay the wild forest and the marshes which Aaku knew like no man else. A few planes came over, dropping bombs at random . . ."

"Kerrump, kerrump."

" . . . but they had no target and did no harm."

Even Lydia's imagination was unwillingly stirred, more by the idea of freedom than by the old hopeless heroisms. She waited for Dickie's inevitable question.

"Is it true, please?"

"Quite true," said Paul, "It was just like that. I was there."

Lydia was faintly irritated by the truthful ring of what she knew to be a lie, and then by the amused glance Paul flashed at her.

"Dickie is a good demonstration of Lysenkoist theory," he said. "The military urge has become hereditable."

"Rubbish," snapped Lydia. "He's been indoctrinated, and by a civilian sawbones at that. Sorry—I didn't mean to sound churlish. He's loved it, haven't you, darling?"

Dickie grunted his thanks, already absorbed in the process of re-settling the paper avalanche on its hillside so that he could fight the whole battle over again. Trevor stirred on Lydia's shoulder and burped so suddenly and violently that he shocked himself into a howl. Like a mother seal rushing to the sound of her pup's voice Mrs Pumice came bowling into the room, looking almost dizzy with happiness.

"Hello!" she cried. "My, you've been busy. Have you been a good boy then, sweetie?"

Trevor's wail rose. Mrs Pumice snatched him from Lydia's arms and made a great but ineffective show of loving him.

"I must go now," said Paul, picking up the pens, and did so before Lydia could thank him. Dickie looked sulky at the disappearance of his train, but in a second or two he had replaced it with an imaginary one which puffed, inaudible through Trevor's crying, between the snow-sprinkled pines.

"I'm glad you found me up here," shouted Lydia. "I wanted to consult you about colour schemes in here."

"It's all right," yelled Mrs Pumice. "I haven't got to move. I've got my back rent, *and* a month in advance."

She dumped Trevor onto the bed, ruining the Livonian landscape. He rolled onto his stomach and crawled towards the scene of the battle, whining. A Mig came over, whining on a different note, and strafed him vigorously. Mrs Pumice took her rent book and a sheaf of money out of her shoulder-bag.

"Five weeks back is twenty-two fifty," she said, "and four in advance is eighteen. That's forty fifty, right?"

She counted the money out in five-pound notes.

"You've found treasure too?" said Dickie. "I found treasure, Mum found treasure, you found treasure. Tack attack attack attack tack."

"You found Ma Newbury's will?" said Mrs Pumice, bright and gossipy. "Was there any money with it? I bet there was."

"Dickie found tuppence under the carpet and I found some family papers of Mrs Newbury's. There isn't a will," said Lydia.

She tried to speak with less coldness than she felt but the tone came out obviously false, and that made her produce one of her classic blushes, scarlet from scalp to collar-bone. Mrs Pumice evidently felt the rebuff, for she answered with sudden aggressiveness.

"You never asked me where my money come from," she said. "Don sent it, more than what he owed."

"That's great."

"So now I haven't got to move. You can't *make* me, can you? It might mean he wants to come back after all, see?"

She stared at Lydia as if challenging her to say it was a lie. Mrs Newbury had used exactly that look to support her more outrageous fibs.

"Well, that's fine," said Lydia. "We'll just leave everybody where they are for the moment, and Mr Vaklins can move into this room, which he wants to do."

"Ooh, that'll be nice," said Mrs Pumice. "Have you seen his car? It's smashing! Well, I'll be seeing you. Tirra, Dickie."

She snatched her child out of Livonia and left. Dickie restored his battlefield to coherence and started the ambush again. Lydia went gloomily back to work, reshaping her ideas as she did so. OK, leave everybody in their existing rooms. If Paul would pay twelve for this one there'd be no need to ask the Pelletiers for any more. Allow another six weeks to get the basement into decent nick, why, she could have started her baby months ago and she'd still have been all right. Some clouds do have silver linings.

12

In the unwilling March sunshine Dickie and Lydia stood under the porch of the white plaster wedding-cake which was 109 Hyde Park Gardens. First Sundays in the month were always the same: she woke with a vague reluctance which increased by midday to a depresion which made lunch seem completely insipid; Dickie, on the other hand, lived in a mounting tornado of activity and excitement; now they both stood under the porch, Dickie skipping from foot to foot even while he pressed the bell, and Lydia feeling as usual like a dark little mouse whose weight on the step would snap the trap shut and cage her for ever.

"Who is it?" crackled Lalage's voice from the speaker by the column of bell pushes.

"The men come to hoover the elephant," cackled Dickie (a new joke, concocted by him and Richard during last night's bed-time session).

"She's been getting a bit dusty," said Lalage. "We're thinking of buying a non-stick elephant. Have you anything in that line?"

"Only non-stick hippo . . . hippo . . ."

Dickie broke down before he could finish the word.

"Well, bring one up," said Lalage. "Don't bust the lift, though."

The door buzzed and opened. In the lift Dickie bounced and thrilled, mercifully unable to sense Lydia's inner shrinking. Lalage was holding the flat door open and he hurtled through it, yelling "Boom, Boom, Kiss me Hardy, Boom, Boom."

"Boom, boom," answered Father's voice from the old nursery. Even in those two syllables Lydia sensed that he was the kindly old scholar this visit. Dickie hurtled through the nursery door.

"Men!" yawned Lalage. "How are you, darling. You look marvellous. I've got a new job."

71

"That's great," said Lydia, relaxing. It was going to be an easy visit, with plenty to talk about and both Father and Lalage in bearable roles. By the time she'd hung her coat on her own peg in the passage Lalage was on the sofa in the drawing room, sprawling luxuriously among the cushions. Lydia settled into her usual small, hardish, constricting chair, opened the sewing-box beside it and took out the tapestry stool-cover that had already seen her through two years of first-Sundays-in-the-month.

"What's the job?"

"London correspondent of a New York glossy business mag. Six thousand a year plus three thousand expenses."

"That sounds perfect."

"Can't you be a *bit* jealous, darling, just to put the cream on my cake."

"But I couldn't begin to do a job like that, let alone like doing it. It's the same as that stupid question about which past age would you prefer to live in. I live now, and that's part of me being me. To live then I'd have to be someone else. To do your job I'd have to be someone else. I'm me, I like it."

Lydia threaded her needle with mauve silk and began to stitch in another line of background between the two stunted chaffinches which were the main feature of the design. It really was becoming gratifyingly hideous. Lalage stretched on the sofa, thinking about money, sensual as Danae under her storm of gold. Lydia stopped stitching and mentally compared her half-sister's prettiness with Procne Newbury's beauty. Lalage's complexion was almost as good, and was set off by her glossy black hair. Her features were small and well-formed too; but there was something deficient in the soft, clear oval of her face, an absence of character, not because Lalage lacked character but because she didn't allow it to appear on the surface to spoil the pretty image. Whereas Procne *was* her own beauty, all through.

"Have you got anything I can wear at a big embassy reception?" asked Lydia.

"Jesus! Which embassy?"

"Russia."

"I'm not lending you my best new Cardin to get all ripped up when you're chucked out. What's it about this time? Exit visas for Jews?"

Lydia laughed.

"I did wonder whether I oughtn't to," she said. "But I've

promised Richard I'll behave. I'll promise you too, if you like."

"Then why are you going at all? You?"

"Oh, it's perfectly stupid. Richard has a friend called George Dunakhov—I like him too—he's like somebody in a Chekhov farce—we knew him when we were at the embassy in Buda and now he's in London and he's got us invited to a big cultural do. In fact I threw the envelope away without opening it, because I thought it was an ad for some shoe-shop or something, but then I fished it out of the waste-paper basket because I needed a bit of card to draw a diagram for a rather thick electrician, and there was this absurd invitation, with a note from George, and at that moment he rang up to check I'd got it. I hadn't time to think of an excuse, and any-way Richard's a bit starved of that sort of function. So what have you got I can wear?"

"Let's go and try a few things on," said Lalage.

They spent almost an hour doing that, while the gunfire of Trafalgar thundered in the nursery and faint whiffs of gunpowder crept under the door to mix with the boudoir odours of Lalage's room.

Tea went very well. Afterwards Dickie decided to watch TV and let Lydia enjoy the privilege of clearing up the battle of Trafalgar. Father, with his characteristic fussy precision, put away his beautifully painted little Airfix models while Lydia swept up the remains of expendable paper ships (Father was very proud of his exploding *Bucentaur*), tidied away the fans which provided the prevailing winds, hoovered the canvas sea and finally rolled it up to expose the old, familiar-stained brown nursery carpet.

"I want a bit of help," she said abruptly.

"Cash?" said Father, sickeningly understanding. "I'm fairly flush just now."

This was recognised family code, and meant that he wasn't spending every penny he earned on some girl with a taste for Ferraris, Krug and the Bahamas.

"No, we're doing OK, thanks," said Lydia. "I've got a new tenant who's paying more for one room than some of them are for four. I want some advice, really."

"Good God!"

"I want to know something about a particular post mortem . . ."

"Which hospital?"

"St Ursula's."

"Might be able to help. I know Crichton-Powell there. What's up?"

"You remember about the old woman who died in my house? The evidence at the inquest was pretty straight-forward—she had a lot of alcohol in her bloodstream and she'd been climbing up on a table to do something to the curtains when she fell and hit her head on the corner of the fender. I want to know whether there's any way of telling how long she'd been drinking for, and also whether there was any other possible interpretation of the evidence."

"Umm—this sounds a bit paranoid, my dear."

"It's not for me. I'm visiting her daughter in prison, and she's absolutely convinced that her mother would never have touched alcohol. I want to get her to accept the facts before *she* becomes paranoid. There's another thing—the old lady left a bit of money behind, and I think there's a chance she'd been cheating her employers out of the booze. It would suit me if she'd only just begun drinking, because that would mean that they hadn't much claim on the money and it could all go to the girl."

"Umm. I do a stint at St Ursula's on Tuesdays. I can't guarantee to bump into Chrichton-Powell, but I'll probably do so before next month. What are the details—name, address and date ought to be enough."

"Mrs Daphne Newbury, my address, died on the night of the 31st of January."

Father was half-way through writing this into his little black pocket-book when his good-samaritan face slipped, creased and became inquisitive and roguish as he turned to stare at her.

"Not little Procne's Mamma?" he said.

"That's right," she snapped.

He pursed his lips, head cocked, speculative. Lydia swallowed.

"Did you know her?" she said.

"We had quite a bit of fun together, once, but then she moved out of my class. How is she?"

"Prison is hell. You can't ask how people in hell are, especially if you helped put them there. But I hope she's going to come and live at Devon Crescent when she gets out."

It was a momentary comfort to see him shocked. It may be amusing, even delightful, for randy old cynics to consort with harlots, but it is certainly improper for the daughters of

74

the cynics to invite harlots into their houses.

"You asked me for some advice, my girl," he said. "I'm going to give you some. Steer clear of Procne Newbury."

"I like her."

"Perhaps. In my experience Procne has no moral sense at all."

"Balls!"

"But I have heard it argued that the question whether she has any moral sense is subsumed into the large question whether she has sense of any kind. She's not merely impulsive—she's an embodied impulse."

"You simply can't judge somebody like that by the way somebody like you knows them."

"Perhaps. I told you she'd moved out of my class. That was only partly true. What really put me off was that she moved in with a group of people I find very frightening indeed. Genuine, hard, violent criminals. There are some men who get an extra kick out of that sort of thing. Not me."

"She didn't move in with them, she was taken over by them. And how's she ever going to get away from them if there's nowhere for her to go to and no one else she knows?"

"Well, I've said my piece."

"OK. Now shut up!"

He sighed and stopped. Grey-hairs-with-sorrow-to-the-grave. Lydia sensed the old appalling useless rage beginning to thresh round and round inside her, battering against the walls of her being like the dying king cobra in *Rikki-tikki-tavi*. At the crisis moment Dickie hurtled into the room brandishing his grandfather's best ebony walking stick.

"Have at you, fat varlet!" he cried, and thwacked his grandfather on the knee.

"Toothache!" he yelled.

"It's been *The Three Musketeers* on the box," said Lalage from the door. "Sometimes he makes me realise how much I've missed, being a girl. I've often longed to do that. Are you all right, darling?"

"By God, I've lost my leg!" gritted Father.

"So you have, by God!" squealed Dickie. "Stand up, Guards! Hard pounding, gentlemen—we'll see who can pound hardest. Boom! Boom!"

He fell on one knee and began to load the walking-stick with an invisible ram-rod. Father lowered himself into a chair and rubbed his knee-cap. Lalage leaned against the door-post, laughing soundlessly with all her teeth showing.

Lydia stood by the window, completely left out, unable even to enjoy Dickie's whirling happiness. Dickie himself in the act of spitting a musket-ball down the barrel of the walking-stick suddenly remembered the other battlefield and reverted to D'Artagnan.

"My turn," said Father, holding out his hand for the lunging stick. "The defeated army needs its crutch to hobble home on."

"Cut it off? Boiling tar?" asked Dickie.

"May not be necessary," said father. "On the other hand, next time you come I might be wearing a peg leg. Time for you to go, isn't it? I'll find out about your old lady, my dear."

"Thanks," said Lydia.

"Goodness, I enjoyed that," said Lalage. "Don't forget the dress, darling—I really ought to give it you, it suits you so well. Look, if I come and collect it some time next week I can see how you're getting on with your upheavals."

The last wash of rage receded. Lydia remembered Richard's idiotic suggestion.

"Come and have supper," she said. "I'll give you a ring. I've got a handsome young ship-owner I'd like you to meet."

It was foolishly gratifying to watch Lalage's eyes widen.

13

LYDIA'S SECOND VISIT to the prison was rather different from the first. It had taken considerable persistence to persuade the authorities to let her come at all, as she was neither a relation nor a technically acceptable visitor. She had kept her cool, recognising that the problem was not official bloody-mindedness, or even lack of goodwill, but just the blind intransigence of the system. However, as Procne had no other visitors, and as Lydia persisted until even the system dimly recognised that she wasn't going to go away, here she was again, waiting in the crowded octagonal room by the gate, feeling almost an old hand.

But the wait was longer than before, and then she was taken not to the pink cell but to a larger room which contained a number of long tables with chairs on either side—something like a library reading-room without any books. Most of the places were occupied by other visitors and other prisoners. Two prison officers invigilated the scene. The room was full of muttering which, even though the words were inaudible, seemed to move in stilted rhythms.

Procne was already waiting, wearing a neutral-coloured overall. She was obviously the prettiest girl in the room (though there was one thin, tiny-headed black girl who might have collected a few votes) but Lydia didn't feel this time as though she was in the presence of something amazing, a different order of creation from all the other people she knew.

"Hi," said Lydia. "How's things?"

"Hi, Liz. Good of you to come."

"I had a bit of trouble persuading them. If you want me to go on coming you've got to ask. You look as though it's been getting you down a bit."

"Get anyone down. I been sleeping badly."

"Is that worry?"

"Nothing to worry about in here, have I? No, it's just

being shut up like this you might as well be dead. Being asleep and being dead's not much different, really. So I don't need the sleep, see?"

"Are you eating OK?"

"Not so bad. But the food! It's not disgusting, like, only it's dead boring, always the same. I used to eat a lot of scampi. First thing I'll do when I get out is to go and buy myself a bloody great plate of scampi."

She fell silent. The mild animation which the imagined taste had raised waned from her features.

"You'll be able to afford it," said Lydia. "I found the money your mother left."

"Did you really? That's great!"

"It's a bit over a thousand pounds."

"Great! Hey, are you sure she meant it for me?"

"There's nothing to show she didn't. I put it in the Post Office in my name, because that seemed easiest, but you can have it as soon as you want."

"You haven't told anyone, have you?" said Procne in a whisper.

"No, of course not. Why?"

"Perhaps if the police found out they'd want it back, pay for them cheques."

"Oh, I don't think so. It was your mother's money, not yours."

"It come from me. Besides . . ."

Her eyes flicked to either side and when she spoke again her voice was even lower.

"That mob I was telling you about, they wouldn't like it. If I got a bit put by, they might think I was trying to get shot of them, see? They keep an eye on what their best girls are doing. There was one of them at my trial, most days."

"I had an idea about all that, Procne. Would you like a room in my house when you come out? The rent's quite low."

"I don't know about that."

"You see, there's two things. They're much more likely to let you out of here, early I mean, on parole, if you've got somewhere to go to—I mean a room of your own, and friends who they think are honest, and a job, and so on."

"Well, I haven't got a job, have I? There's only one thing I can do."

"Rubbish. You'd make a marvellous model, and you could use some of your mother's money to pay for a course. I think

I could easily set up a job for you if you wanted—I mean a proper job you'd be really interested in doing . . ."

"I don't know."

"Well, think about it . . . look, I'm not trying to tell you what to do—that's your own business. Only I don't want you to feel that you've got to go back to living the way you did because that's all there is for you to do. If you want to, that's fine. But if you want to try something else, I think I could help."

"It's been my own fault, really. Just it always seems the easiest thing, so I string along. Then when this mob . . . Honest, Liz, you'd better keep out of it. You don't know them."

"I can cope. They've got where they are because people are scared to stand up to them. Somebody's got to, some time. I'm in a better position than most. The important thing is that you should have the choice open to you."

"Sometimes it's best not to have no choice, then it isn't your fault, see?"

"Well, there's plenty of time . . . damn! what a stupid thing to say. I found out about the vodka."

"Bet she wasn't drinking none."

Lydia explained about the *varosh*, and the regular order at the off-licence. Procne shook her head.

"Never!" she said. "Oh, she'd have nicked the booze and not turned a hair, provided she'd got someone she could flog it to. But empties in her room, never! I told you last time about what she did with Dad's empties?"

"Yes, you did. I had one possible idea—suppose your mother sometimes found a little in the bottom of one of the bottles—the old men are pretty clumsy with it—they spilt a whole jugful last month. Don't you think she might have started to collect those dregs . . ."

"Pity to waste that," said Procne. The imitation of her mother's voice was so accurate that Lydia was side-tracked.

"Can you do that with other people?" she asked. "I mean could you do me?"

"I'd have to have a bit of practice. I got one la-di-da voice I do, but it ain't quite right for you. My dear girls, I have come here to-day to talk to you about the joys of crochet-work."

"Oh dear. I hope that's not me."

"Course not. You got a way of biting your words off short, specially when you're angry. Snip snap, that's that,

79

anyone else want a thorough dusting over? No, that's not it, it's only the top bit, not all that happiness you got inside you. Your husband's a lucky man, Liz."

"I gave him a nervous breakdown three years ago—or at least I helped to give it him."

"Don't you believe it—he'd of had it worse with anyone else."

"I'm sorry. I don't normally tell people. What were we talking about?"

"Oh, me doing voices. I'll have a bit of practice at yours—I can do all the screws, and the governors—passes the time, see?"

"I think it's marvellous. I'm sure you could use it, too. But I meant before that—suppose your mother had collected about a bottle, and she suddenly felt depressed, or ill. Suppose she persuaded herself that the vodka counted as medicine . . ."

Procne shook her head.

"No, Mum weren't never ill," she said. "You'd of had to lay her out before you could make her touch a drop. Why, weddings she always used to take her own Thermos of tea to toast the bride in."

"Well, what do you think happened?"

"Someone done her in," whispered Procne.

"Why should they?"

"Find that money, of course. Or perhaps . . . yes, look, Liz, she was ever so nosey. I told you we used to have a long chat on the phone, Thursdays, and I told her how I was doing and all? Well, I don't remember but I expect I told her quite a bit about the mob what I was working for. Suppose she thought she might try a bit of blackmail? They wouldn't of stood for that, but she wouldn't of known. They'd rub her out, easy as winking, wouldn't they?"

Lydia decided to go along with the fantasy. Procne evidently had all her mother's relish for melodrama, and there was no point in spoiling her fun by raising any of the obvious practical objections.

"You'd better not tell anyone, Procne," she said. "I mean, if you're right, you don't want to get it into the grapevine."

"Or I'll tell you what," said Procne, ignoring her. "Them old gentlemen, they got something hid up there. There's rooms they wouldn't never let her into."

"I've been into all their rooms," said Lydia.

"But you're not nosey, like what she was. They got *secrets*."

"Yes, I suppose so," said Lydia, sighing mentally at those mummified Baltic intrigues. "Anyway, I'll see if I can find out some more. I'll remind my bloody father . . ."

"Why don't you get along with him, Liz? You sound worse than what I was with Mum. What's your mother like?"

"She died when I was eight. I think she killed herself but I've never had the guts to find out. She divorced my father when I was four."

"That's why . . . you and your Dad, I mean?"

"We've always fought. It was worst when Richard decided to leave the army. But we get along now in a sort of way, like most people. Anyway, I'll remind him to find out about that autopsy. The trouble is, with a house like mine it's only too easy for a stranger to get in and out."

"There you are then. Only you be careful too, Liz. Don't go nosing around. It isn't worth it. Tell me about your little boy."

Dickie lasted them until the half hour was up. In a few last gabbled sentences they made arrangements for another visit and Procne promised to think about whether she wanted a room at Devon Crescent. Lydia walked to the tube, buffeted by the dusty gusts of a dry spring wind and depressed by the knowledge of the odds against her bringing off what she wanted to achieve for Procne. But by the time she was sitting in the clanging train she was already so busy with plans for reducing the odds that she was humming loud enough to make the bloke sitting opposite her keep glancing at her over his paper.

14

IT WAS IMPOSSIBLE not to think of Mr Roberts as 'The Spy' still. There was something about him that kept the absurd charade alive, and actually made Lydia slightly jumpy when he came in for morning coffee, in case she should accidentally say something which let on that he had a two-fold existence, if only in her mind. The trouble was that it wasn't pure charade—there were several silly little details which kept making links with the real world, not strong enough to bear the weight of any deduction, but teasingly there. He was too good a gardener, and too hard a worker, for one thing. It was quite unnatural that a casual labourer, engaged by impulse, should be such a treasure. He was a stock little man in his late fifties, with a rather soft and completely humorless pale face, but Lydia was still genuinely not certain that he was the same man she'd bumped into in the basement doorway. She had quite a strong mental picture of that other man —taller and thinner with heavy eyebrows—but again she wasn't wholly sure that this wasn't her imagination. Finally there was his conversation. He had, or affected, a peasant-like reserve. When Lydia said anything, however provocative, he would appear to think about it in silence for several seconds. Then he would agree with her, usually repeating her words in a flat, unplaceable accent. Often she wasn't even certain that he understood what he was saying. The style of assent was almost theatrically sage, but sometimes she felt it was a technique for preserving his own privacy as an urban solitary; sometimes for concealing his real trade as a spy; and sometimes just an instinctive method of disguising stupidity.

At his second visit he had asked quite a lot of questions about the other occupants of the house, what their families were and how long they'd been there, but had shown no interest at all in the Government—in fact he had almost ostentatiously avoided talking about them. Yet another thing was

that Mrs Tevell had told Lydia that he was a frightful old
gossip, though that may have been only her way of describ-
ing a good listener. At any rate, he made Lydia nervous.

On a soft Monday morning in the third week of March
they stood side by side at the top of the steps leading up into
the back garden from the basement. Their mugs steamed
in their hands. Birds trilled, buds glistened in the precocious
and deceitful sunlight. The fresh-dug earth in front of them,
though, seemed to smell still of winter, clammy and chill.

"I can't tell you how glad I am to see the last of those roses,
Mr Roberts," said Lydia. "I hated them. They had a few
mangy flowers in summer and looked hideous for the rest
of the year."

"Weren't much good," agreed Mr Roberts.

"What shall we do with the bushes? The dustmen are a bit
bolshie about collecting rubbish, especially if it's got thorns
on."

"Well, yes, there's thorns," admitted Mr Roberts.

"Are they too wet to burn?"

"They're wet enough."

"Anyway, let's try. I've got some bits of spare timber you
could use to start a bonfire—I kept them to show the dry-rot
people, but they weren't interested. And I'll find you a couple
of planks to put down by the wall there, so that Mrs Pelletier
can get at her washing-line."

"Ah."

"It seems a pity to get a good fire going just for a few old
rose bushes. I wonder whether there's anything worth burning at Mrs Tevell's or any of the others. We could get rid of
it all in one go."

"Ah."

This grunt seemed even more non-committal than the last.
Did it go against his training as a spy to admit that he kept
reserves of garden rubbish elsewhere? Did he regard his
dealings with his other employers' rubbish as a private matter? Was he simply too thick to grasp the advantages of a
communal bonfire? Lydia stared at the neat patch where the
roses had been, suddenly oppressed by the knowledge that
now she'd have to decide what to put into it. One half of her
longed for flagstones, trouble-free tubs of annuals, a tree
for summer shade; the other half wanted jungle, wildness
and freedom in the urban barracks.

"Would a passion-flower grow here, Mr Roberts?"

"Passion-flower. Ah."

"I don't mean in the bed—I mean up the back of the house."

He turned and stared up at the white façade, so much less regular, but somehow more pleasing, than the front. Lydia followed his gaze. There was a smear all down the clean Snocem from one of the drain-pipes—Mrs Evans had blocked her sink outlet again. Bloody woman. It was really quite extraordinary that somebody who could turn herself out so neatly and behave, socially, with such precise decorum, should fail to grasp that a mixture of tea-leaves, potato-peelings and grease was bound to block a sink outlet.

Higher up a head craned out of a window gazing down at the garden, motionless, a live gargoyle. It was Count Linden, but he didn't answer Lydia's wave. The spy appeared not to notice him.

"Ah, a passion flower," he said. "That'll grow all right. Right old nuisance you'll find it, too. *And* you'll have to restrict its roots, or you won't get no flowers."

"Restrict its roots?" said Lydia, changing roles so that she echoed what he said.

"Ah," said the spy. "Squash 'em in tight. That's right."

It was only in the spy-fantasy that he seemed to be speaking about Count Linden, and thinking of little Livonia. It would be the season of thaw in the Baltic republics now, the time (Mr Obb had once said) when the whole world seemed new and beautiful, full of beginnings.

"I'll think about it," said Lydia.

He made a very effective bonfire, got the roses burning, fetched hedge clippings and Michaelmas daisy stalks from other gardens, swept up every leaf in the back garden (in London new drifts of leaf-fall seem to accumulate all winter) and burnt them too. Not once, as ordinary gardeners do, did he stop working to gaze into the smoking pile, as if searching in the twirling white streams for portents and omens. Before he went he shovelled the hot ashes onto the rose-bed, forked them around and raked them in.

If you thought of him as a gardener he was a jewel, Lydia agreed with her neighbours. But if you thought of him as a spy his efficiency was frightening. When he had gone the rosebed had the look of a patch sown with salt, deliberately, so that nothing should ever grow there.

15

"CAPTAIN SIR RICHARD TIMMS and Lady Timms," bawled the bloke. As always at this moment Lydia blushed, not with shyness but with shame at the ridiculous tag which an accident of love had wished on her. The Russian Ambassador and his wife both looked as though they had been deliberately bred to conform to a new module of humanity, perhaps designed to colonise a planet with greater gravity than earth's, as they were stocky and extraordinarily short-necked. The Ambassador took Lydia's hand and bent as if to kiss it, but then seemed to recoil from such a revision of Marxist-Leninist etiquette and compromised with a pudgy, lingering squeeze. Lydia had a sudden lust to kick him on the knee-cap and see what happened, but that would have been impossible in the ridiculous crimson tube which Lalage had coaxed her into wearing.

She and Richard passed on, took glasses of champagne from a tray, and drifted into the muttering throng. The atmosphere was familiar from diplomatic days. It always reminded Lydia of the congregation in a church before a big posh wedding, crowds of people who know each other well and long to give glad cries and swap family scandal, but are forced by the semi-sanctity of the occasion into small gestures and whispered talk. Then George Dunakhov barged between two groups of silvery First Secretaries like a tank coming out of a birch wood. He buffeted Richard on the shoulder and hugged Lydia so firmly to his unyielding chest that she felt that she would be branded for the rest of her life with a vertical row of little red stars where the buttons of his uniform dug into her

"Hoi, hoi," he bellowed. "Now I see it is worth I come to England!"

He was drunk already.

"George will never stay the course, unless there's a war," Richard had once said. "Suddenly they'll get tired of him, and then, puff. If there's a war he'll do well—he's a bloody good tank commander."

But here he was still beating the system somehow. Lydia would have liked him for that alone. He let go of her, but grabbed her hand and towed her at high speed through the crowd to a table by the wall. Naturally he'd already set himself up with the necessities of life—two bottles of champagne, spare glasses and a smiling huge-bosomed blonde in a green dress. With exaggerated gestures, like a pimp in a baroque comedy, George introduced her. Her name was Natya, plus one of those impossibly amnemonic Russian surnames. She preferred to speak French.

Before they'd settled a tall, dark-skinned young man strolled up and found himself sucked into the tornado of George's hospitality. His name was Nikolai Diarghi. He worked at the Embassy and spoke perfect English.

George immediately began to tell the blonde a shooting story, remotely based on something that had actually happened to him and Richard in Hungary. In the middle of a train of surreal improbabilities he would stop and ask Richard to confirm some small irrelevant detail, as if taking up an everyday parcel at a little way-side halt, before steaming on through the landscape of his fantasy.

"Do you find much shooting in England, Lady Timms?" said Mr Diarghi, deliberately drawing her out of George's audience.

"We don't live that sort of life nowadays. Richard is reading for the bar and I look after a large house and a small boy."

"A small boy? Ah, I wonder if you can help me. I am preparing a report on the British nursery education system. Of course I have access to all sorts of official views, but it is hard for me to make contact with ordinary mothers of small children. Do you have any views on the subject?"

Poor man. It was as if Moses had struck the rock and out gushed Niagara. Lydia's views on nursery education were precise and vehement. For six months in the previous year she had been one of an action group who were trying to coax or force the ILEA into opening a new nursery school in her area, and had resigned when she discovered that most of her colleagues really wanted it as a convenience for the Lady Timmses of W.11 and not as a life-line for the Mrs Pumices. She was still talking when the flunkey bawled for silence. The Ambassador made an oily little speech of welcome. Everybody started to move towards another room.

"I didn't realise we were going to be fed," said Lydia.

"Oh, yes," said Mr Diarghi. "Excuse me. Dunakhov will know where you sit. I'd like to carry on with our conversation, so I'll just nip ahead and see if I can fiddle the seating plan."

It was a vast, slow meal, with speeches and toasts between the courses. The object of the reception was to celebrate a big cultural-exchange deal between the two countries, and the British speakers—politicians, diplomats, art administrators—seemed to Lydia even suaver and more hypocritical than the Russians. Only one knighted actor even faintly hinted at the lives that might be crushed, the truth that might be poisoned in order that the garden of Russian culture should bloom as its owners wished. His speech was especially well received, being neatly within the limits of polite protest and thus serving as the token conscience of authority. But for her promise to Richard Lydia would have thrown her plate at the purring sir. Instead, when talk and eating restarted, she loosed her rage on poor George.

He smiled, shrugged and began another of his stories. Lydia was already a bit irritated with him, because she'd decided that the real reason for their being there was that George wanted to show off his baronet to his blonde. When she swung away from him in mid sentence Mr Diarghi neatly fielded her diatribe.

"Yes," he said when she ran out of breath. "Have you been in Bombay, or any place where there are many beggars?"

"No."

"It is horrible, but it is also a parable. Along the streets where the rich men go they line the paving, like soldiers guarding a state visit. Each has his own pitch, and each has his own hideous defect—he is blind, she has a withered arm, that child has no legs, that old man a great sore that suppurates. No, I am not changing the subject. My point is that the idea, in that context, of a healthy beggar is a contradiction in terms. In the present context of the world—the stage we have reached in the historical process—the idea of a government that does not crush some individuals is a contradiction in terms. They all must do it, and in that case it is clearly more satisfactory to have a government that knows who it is crushing, and why."

"I don't think I accept any of that," said Lydia, too earnest to eat. "I don't accept that governments have to crush people. Suppose they do, though, I don't accept that it's better for them to be aware of what they're doing, because that sanctions the repression and makes it officially OK. And even if it were better, it's still vital that people shouldn't accept it. Once you start shrugging your shoulders whenever somebody gets trampled on, then the stupid government engine begins to think that no one minds. *It* had no feelings, you see. So it tramples where it likes. Look, as a Marxist you're supposed to be working towards a perfect government, so it matters even more that you should have the imperfections shown up, by people like me, if there's no one else to do it."

Mr Diarghi nodded but said nothing.

"How long would *I* survive in Russia?" she asked.

"If you started throwing plates at distinguished speakers at official functions?"

"I wouldn't get asked again, but what else?"

"Well, you would survive your natural span, of course, but perhaps if you disturbed the ideas of too many people it might be necessary to restrain you. But remember, if you think that an injustice, that you have to balance it against the far greater injustice of the millions of people in capitalist countries whose lives the system makes ugly and stunted, but who would be allowed to thrive under our system."

"By restrain me you mean send me to a lunatic asylum, or to a labour camp?"

"If necessary."

"Are you seriously telling me that I'd live to a ripe old age in Siberia?"

"Most people do—in fact some remain active to an extraordinary old age—Aaku Aakisen is a good example."

Lydia was about to argue when the plates were cleared and a Russian rose to reply to the actor with a speech so inept and boring that it seemed to dim even the chandeliers. Lydia could sense the dust settling on distinguished pates, the infection of dullness creeping, like one of the Devon Crescent fungi, from mind to mind. George was not the only guest snoring. When at last the man sat down to a round of muffled clapping she found that she no longer had any gusto for a political set-to.

"I didn't know that you acknowledged Aakisen's existence," she said.

"Oh yes. His name came to mind because I've just read a

report of his death in a CIA propaganda sheet, but it's surprising that you've heard of him. The attempt to make propaganda with his death was very ineptly handled."

"Oh dear. All that effort wasted. I printed his obituary notice for the Livonian, er, Consulate. They live on the top two floors of my house. I'm their landlady, and I'm the only person who seems able to manage their duplicating machine. In fact there's a bloke baby-sitting for me at the moment who probably told my son a bed-time story about Aakisen."

"What a coincidence that I should mention him! How do you reconcile your views on authority with your giving shelter to a so-called Government in exile?"

"Oh, they were there when I bought the house. Anyway, I don't think much of any governments, but at least I prefer ones which have been chosen by the people they govern. I rather like the Livs—they're a lot of harmless old dreamers, kind and sad."

"Their dreams are nightmares, Lady Timms. The so-called Balkan Republics have had a difficult history, but it is a mistake to treat them all as one. I personally admire and respect the Estonians, for instance, even the ones who have come into exile. But I do not care for the Livs. Listen, you have three old men in your house, I think. Busch, Linden and . . . I've forgotten his name."

"Mr Obb."

"Obb. A quiet man, I believe, a survivor. He would be living in Livonia still if he had not collaborated a little too freely with the Nazis, but otherwise I know nothing against him. Busch and Linden, though . . . During the war of 1919-20 (which, by the way, is still the root cause of Russian suspicion of the motives of the European powers) Busch led a cavalry regiment. There was a period when our Revolutionary Army was in retreat, under attack from the so-called White Russians, together with French and British troops and units from the Balkan States. Where Busch's regiment came, they killed every Russian they found, man, woman and child. Some they tortured first. This was on his personal orders."

"But . . ."

"Let me finish. There has always been a strong German influence in the Baltic States. Most of the great landowners were Germans by origin and allegiance. For instance, Linden's family owned larger estates than many of your English dukes, in a country one tenth of the size. The people who lived on his land were worse protected even than our Russian serfs. His grandfather had powers of life and death—not legal powers, but he exercised them. That is the Livonia Linden fought for . . . no, he wasn't a soldier, but during the Nazi invasion he was a very active collaborator. He took charge of a programme to export all Livonian Jews to Germany, to the extermination camps. He also organised a squad of internal terrorists, on the Nazi side, to eliminate difficult citizens—they had many little techniques. It was quite noticeable, for instance, that a number of Linden's political opponents died very suddenly from what appeared to be heart stoppages. He was extremely zealous. Even if all the stories you read in your British papers were true, Lady Timms, we Russians have done nothing to the Jews remotely comparable to the actions of this man you now have living under your roof."

Somebody had put a many-coloured hill of ice-cream in front of Lydia. Nuggets of scented chocolate were buried in its slopes. She took a vague spoonful and licked at it. It seemed to have no taste at all. She suddenly remembered Count Linden leaning from the back of her own house, staring down at the patch of fresh-dug earth. In her memory, for a moment, he became visibly a monster—almost fanged, almost bat-winged—before she shook herself and asserted that it had been a pretty March morning and Linden no more than a grey old man leaning out of a window. The ice-cream acquired flavour.

"You mustn't think I'm just making propaganda," said Mr Diarghi. "You'll find an account of Busch's activities in a report by Colonel Tallents, in volume three of the *British Foreign Policy Documents*, 1919-39, First Series. And several times shortly after the war there were questions about Linden in your House of Commons. I can send you the Hansard references if you want to look them up."

Still Lydia said nothing.

"I'm sorry," said Mr Diarghi, smiling. "This isn't really dinner-party conversation."

"It's all right," said Lydia. "I mean, I'd much rather talk about things like this than the weather. OK, send me those references—though I wouldn't accept them as proof. There's always a bunch of MPs who'll ask any kind of question at all if they think it'll embarrass the government—they don't have to be in your pay for that."

"You'll be hard to convince of anything you don't want to believe."

90

"So's everyone, and quite right too," snapped Lydia. "Sorry—don't let's get onto that—it's just another of my hobby-horses—I mean, you have to trust your emotions a bit about anything that matters—where were we? Oh, yes, it doesn't make any difference to me if everything you say about my Livs is true. The only possible way to behave is to take people as they are now—they're part of your life and you're part of theirs, and you've got to accept that. It doesn't matter what they were or what they've done. Obviously, there are a few people who've got to be restrained, prevented from repeating anti-social sorts of behaviour, but they're far fewer than any of our societies makes out. And . . . well, for instance, what Israel did to Eichmann was by any standards vile. It didn't matter by then what *he'd* done. That had been vile too, but it was over, finished, unalterable."

Mr Diarghi shook his head.

"You are what I was taught at school to call a Utopian," he said. "Pragmatically I can't see that it would be possible to organise anything but a small group of like-minded people on your beliefs. We are all prisoners of what has happened and what has been done, by ourselves, by our enemies, by our friends. For instance, your late Foreign Secretary maintained a very consistent line for over thirty years about the Baltic States. He invested a great deal of face in their independence. While he was in office it was technically impossible for us to come to any kind of agreement about our *de jure* sovereignty over the areas. Even now there are difficulties. For instance, the Americans pay these Consulates interest on the gold reserves which they hold for them, and this contributes marginally to the British balance of payments. It seems to us that the British Government, thirty years ago, contrived a bribe to itself, and is now trapped by having taken it so long. And so on. You could trace through six hundred years the causes that have brought your old men to live in your two top floors."

"Yes, but most of the causes don't matter any more. And what you told me about Busch and Linden would only matter if there was any chance of their going back to Livonia to form a Government. Then it would at least matter that the voters knew about it . . ."

"It's already well-known in Livonia."

"I bet it isn't known to be true. I've got a friend who went on a lecture tour in Poland, talking to senior schools about the economics of developing countries. One of his lectures had a bit to do with Vietnam—this was before the Americans pulled out—and he gave a fairly factual account of how the war was fought—napalm on villages, defoliation, all that—and he noticed that the kids always smiled at that point. One day he managed to get alone with some of them and ask why. 'Oh,' they said, 'we know you've got to tell a few lies like that or they wouldn't let you in.' "

"Poles," said Mr Diarghi. "Even when you deal straight with them they still manage to cheat themselves."

"Tell me about Aakisen," said Lydia. "What's the truth? Richard says he was probably caught or killed just after the war, and my friends kept him alive for propaganda purposes. I don't know why I should care, but I've got an obsessive sort of feeling that it matters."

Mr Diarghi hesitated.

"I was only quoting the Livonian propaganda as an example," he said. "It may be true, and if it is that would be possible to ascertain from labour camp records. But if Aakisen died, or disappeared—which he may have chosen to do deliberately—then I don't see how anybody can ever be sure. Lady Timms, I have been a little indiscreet in some of the things I have said. I'd prefer not to be quoted, especially to your Livs. This is not my subject, not my area of responsibility. I'm most grateful to you for your help about nursery education, though, and I may well be in touch with you again."

Poor sod, thought Lydia. As soon as he lets his hair down he gets frightened. What a system!

"OK," she said. "I've enjoyed this do a lot more than I expected. Except . . . oh, God, not another one!"

The plates had been cleared again and an English diplomat rose to make a speech of skilled elegance and emptiness. George was woken from his snooze by the applause, and seemed to be at least half sober now. In fact he became attentive and amusing, while Mr Diarghi talked to the woman on his far side. At one moment Richard caught Lydia's eye with a glance of despair; he had the blonde to himself; she laughed, smiled, leaned forward as if offering him some object for inspection on the jutting ledge of her decolletage, reached with smooth bare arms for grapes . . . poor Richard. The act made him almost comically jumpy. He kept raising his right hand to run it through his thinning gingery hair, then failing to complete the movement.

"George," whispered Lydia. "Be a dear and rescue my husband."

George glanced to his right like an anarchist conspirator in a cartoon. His face became immensely serious. He picked up a napkin, folded it into a big triangle, and with a movement of great deftness draped it across the blonde's upper slopes and tied the points behind her neck. She looked at him in momentary astonishment. He put on a parson's face and said something in heavily nasalised Russian. She pealed with laughter like a harlot in a bar near closing-time, a false, hysteric whoop. Richard's relief was so obvious that Lydia and a couple on the far side of the table laughed too. Stirred by this instant of real pleasure amid the desert hours a middle European rose and proposed a toast whose gist seemed to be that cultural exchanges should consist mainly of nudes, which he called nekkid vimmin. He was drunk, and presumably not on the official list of speakers, but several Englishmen were sufficiently far gone to start shouting "Hear, hear," in plummy voices, which George and other irresponsible foreigners parodied with gusto. Lydia tingled with delight at the way, even here, at an event which had been deliberately sealed and sterilised to prevent any such thing happening, life somehow thrust its green blade through.

Mr Diarghi drove them home at nearly two in the morning, but (thank heavens) refused to come in for a nightcap. Paul Vaklins was sitting at the kitchen table soldering a join in a hairy-looking bit of apparatus.

"Welcome to the Resistance Group," he said. "Dickie and I have been building a secret transmitter."

He pressed a key and produced a quick burst of morse.

"It's quite a short-range," he said. "I've fitted suppressors so that it won't interfere with anyone's TV. I'll fix a tape-recorder my end, so that he can get answers to his messages."

"Will he be able to cope with Morse?" said Richard. "He's not really reading yet."

"He might, though," said Lydia. "His reading problem seems to be mainly a visual block."

"He made a damn good start this evening," said Paul. "He's as keen as mustard."

"I think it's a marvelous idea," said Lydia. "It might be

a real way round his problem, especially if I've got to learn Morse along with him."

"The spy sat on the mat," said Richard.

They all laughed, said good-night and went to bed.

16

"A very curious beano," said Richard meditatively. "A very rum occasion indeed."

When you are used, as the Timmses were, to going to bed well before midnight your metabolism seems to slow down when it recognises the time, even though you are still wide awake. Then your bed, when you at last slide into it, seems extra cold. The Timmses did not own an electric blanket and Richard hated hot-water bottles, so now they lay extra close, for warmth. Lydia could feel the tension all along his limbs, though she herself felt happy and relaxed.

"I enjoyed myself after all," she said. "Apart from those ghastly speeches. That Diarghi bloke—well, I suppose anyone who listens to me and takes me seriously seems brainy to me —he told me rather a nasty thing about the Government, though."

"Which Government?"

"Ours. I mean our own. I mean this one here. I mean the Livonians."

She explained about the Livonian atrocities.

"Umm," he said. "That's curious too. Hell, suppose it's true, does it bother you? You're the one who has to cope with them."

"We argued about that, too. I told him it didn't, but it does. I know it oughtn't to, but I can't help it."

"Umm. How did you get onto the subject?"

"I can't remember. We started talking about nursery education, because he's writing a report on that, and then—oh, yes, it was after that actor's speech, we got onto personal freedom and how long people who got sent to Siberia lived, and he produced Aakisen as an example. He knew quite a bit about the Livs, too."

"Umm."

"Don't keep saying 'Umm' like that, as though it all meant

something. Tell me about George's blonde. She looked a toughie, I thought."

"Bang on. That's what she is, if I've got the right girl. Do you remember Jake Seidlitz?"

"Darling, she can't be that girl."

"I don't know. I saw the photographs, and she's just like."

"You never showed me the photographs."

"They were part of a secret film some ass made to warn British businessmen what to expect in Moscow. They'd blacked out Jake's face, but everybody knew. And I saw an FO dossier on her a bit later, when she'd got promoted and was running her own show in East Berlin—same line of business, but with some other girls and a couple of lads to cater for different tastes—so what the hell's she doing as a cultural attaché in London?"

"And throwing her charms around so freely in front of you? Perhaps she was simply keeping in practice. I thought she was just George's girl and he'd got us asked to show her what nobby friends he had. I was pretty disgusted with him at one point."

"Turn but a stone and start a snob. George . . . now there's another thing . . . how sloshed was he?"

"About half-gone to begin with, and three-quarters by the fish. Only about a quarter at the end—those speeches were pretty sobering."

"Umm. You know he's supposed to be in Damascus, training Syrians in tank tactics? I got it out of him. He'd only been there a couple of months, too. And at a kulturfest! George! How much did your chap actually know about nursery education?"

"I did the talking. He kept his end up."

"More than that? Sensible questions?"

"Yes, but not many. Why?"

"Umm. Look, it's probably only glands, or the Law of Real Property maddening me with dullness . . . but when that woman kept brandishing her bust at me . . . and George goes to sleep and wakes up at just the right moments . . . and you're sat next to a chap who starts by triggering you off on one of your hobby-horses . . ."

"Mixed metaphor."

"No, you start hobby-horse races with a popgun. On your sticks, get set, pop . . . and then he drags Aakisen in and he knows all about Livs and he tells you horror stories . . . Diarghi's a Georgian name, I think . . ."

96

"At least he pretty well admitted Aakisen did die in Siberia."

"Umm."

"Come off it, darling. You never really believed in FCPs, even when we lived in that world."

(Most of the Timmses' diplomatic stint had been done at a time when the Foreign Office had been riddled with red scares, and junior staffs had explained all crises—shortage of tonic-water, the Ambassador's daughter's pony going down with equine flu, and so on—as Fiendish Communist Plots.)

"You get trapped by your past, don't you? Now it's impossible for us to believe that anything that happens could conceivably be engineered by the Russians, even though we've got an anti-communist government run from our house. My notion was it might be a bit of a probing operation, George brought over from Syria to get us to the party at all, bloke told off to get you going on schools and then slip in a few horror stories about the Livs, girl imported to see whether there's any leverage to be got from me . . . she'll have to put in a nil return, poor thing."

"You've just got more refined tastes than she's usually asked to cater for. Kiss me?"

"Not just now, thanks."

"I feel all soft and gooey."

"Well I feel like an overwound alarm-clock in a badly assembled time bomb."

"I could kill that woman."

"Oh, it isn't her. I mean, if it is, that's all happening in cupboards I never open. I just feel that we've got about as much on our plate as we can cope with, you in particular, and if somebody starts mucking you up just now I shall go round the bend again."

"But why should they? Why us? Why now?"

"When does the Government's lease run out?"

"First of October, this year."

"I wonder if they know . . . they might. Suppose they either blackmailed me or horrified you into deciding not to renew the lease, that'd mean that the Government would have to try and set up elsewhere, and that might mean the FO had to reconsider the whole question of their diplomatic status. Now old Alec's no longer Foreign Secretary, it'd be a good time for the Russians to put a bit of pressure on. They might even try to show that the Government's been up to some sort of dirty work . . . currency fiddling or something . . . I expect they're working on that already . . ."

"Seriously?"

"Yes. No. It's probably only my imagination. I wish I hadn't got those bloody exams coming up—I never used to have exam nerves . . ."

"But you know it all, darling. You can do it easily."

"Provided I don't go to pieces. Hell!"

Clearly it was a moment to switch the talk back to the FCP.

"But George," said Lydia. "He wouldn't let himself be used, just like that, would he? Bait? He's our friend."

"Darling, if you think about it honestly you'll see that you've got two sorts of friends, ones you like and ones you trust. Sometimes they overlap, not always. I like old George very much, but I'm quite sure he'd slit our throats if he needed to."

This business about liking and trusting was an old argument, so safe in Richard's present state. She let him ramble through a list of all the people they knew, putting them into one category or the other, a soothing game.

"It's more marked with you," he said. "It's natural to feel you can trust people from your own caste, but you don't approve of your own caste, so you tend not to like them."

"Balls. Anyway, I think you're wrong about George. He's not part of an FCP, or if he is he hasn't been told. I suppose there's just a chance you might be right about the rest of it —it *was* a bit odd, in some ways . . ."

"About ten to one against, I'd say."

"Do you think I ought to warn Mr Obb?"

"Umm. You actually want them to stay? What Diarghi told you is probably true—he sounds too bright to tell you fibs you could check."

"Of course I do. I mean, even if I'd been wanting to get them out before, I'd dig my heels in if I thought we were being pushed around by the bloody Kremlin, whatever they'd done, almost. Damn. The idea makes me so angry I'm beginning to become ungooey."

Richard laughed but still didn't really relax. They lay and talked almost till dawn.

17

THE DINNER-PARTY for Lalage went very well at first. Lydia often felt that the only mystery in cooking is why so many cook-book-writers, however inspirational, are quite unable to string together a series of clear and unambiguous sentences. She relied on half a dozen books which understood that a recipe is no more than an assembly instruction; with these she found she could produce good meals with no sweat. Taking the whole day off from building operations she shopped; got the silver out of the bank; improvised a table out of two tea-chests, a door and a sheet of hardboard; pinned up about thirty of Dickie's gaudy battle-pictures to cover the patched and mottled walls of the back room; and there, by the time Dickie came back from school, was a dining-room where yesterday had been a desert. He was thrilled with his art gallery and spent the hours until his bed-time touching in a few more explosions and dead bodies and dive-bombers.

The wine was no problem, because Richard had inherited some, which he kept with a wine-merchant in the City and refused to sell, though somebody had once told Lydia it would fetch twenty quid a bottle. As she wasn't allowed to convert it into floor-boards or stair-carpets she got a certain kick out of simply knocking the stuff back; to drink it like that was an acceptable sort of revenge on a society that had got its values so crazy as to price a bottle of plonk higher than a week's social security payments.

Richard put Dickie to bed. They now had a night-time ritual which involved an adventure behind enemy lines and the use of Paul's Morse transmitter to get the vital message through; it had barely finished its last sleepy beep when Lalage arrived carrying a box of chocolates as big as a tombstone. The other guests were a married couple who lectured in anthropology at London University, Paul Vaklins, and a strange pair, unmarried, who lived in a basement across the road and sent a small girl who didn't seem to be their own child to Dickie's school. They ran an ornamental leather stall in the Portobello Road and turned up for the party wearing identical caftans. Another oddness about them was that they were both devoted workers for the local Tories. Lydia had only asked them on impulse, the morning she'd rung up the Russian embassy and learnt that George had already been posted back to Damascus, but they made a good mix, and the party went well and easily until Lydia, coming back from the kitchen with Richard's favourite pudding (which was a mound of sweetened cream cheese piled with pears soaked in claret) noticed that an extra guest had arrived.

He announced himself as a softness in the shadows, half-seen disturbing shapes in Dickie's dim-lit pictures, a shimmer in the candle-flames, a mutter under the talk, a vapour creeping from the wine. He was Eros.

When Lalage had been only fourteen she had first stolen one of Lydia's blokes, a rather thick lock forward called Pete, just to show that she could. She'd done the same several times since, usually letting the poor sod down with a bump as soon as she'd thoroughly spoilt things. She'd even tried Richard once, but to the best of Lydia's belief had got nowhere. So, though the purpose of the party had been to interest Paul and Lalage in each other, when it happened—happened like that, with an intense flow of invisible energies between them, strong enough to disrupt the talk and make the male anthropologist knock his wine-glass over—the memory of all those old insults rose against Lydia's teeth like vomit. She pressed her lips hard together and spooned the pears out in angry dollops. When she saw Richard, oblivious, smiling at something the female caftan-wearer was telling him she almost slung his pear and cheese in his face.

After that the evening became thoroughly sour for a while, and was made no better when they moved next door for coffee by Paul's attempt to behave decently and accept the re-shuffle of talking-partners. But Lalage broke that up and it was a relief when she suddenly sprang a migraine, too agonising for it to be safe for her to drive herself. Paul gravely accepted the charade and took her home.

"That's quite a large car," said Richard as they watched the tail-lights fade. "I wonder if they'll wait to reach a bed."

Lydia kicked him as hard as she could on the shin.

"Hi! What was that for?"

"I didn't think you'd even noticed. The bloody little bitch!"

"But I thought that was the object of the exercise."

"And she's left that bloody dress behind."

"And her car. Cheer up, she'll get a parking ticket in the morning. That'll be something."

Lydia laughed, found and squeezed his hand and allowed herself to be led back to talk genteelly to the other guests till midnight.

18

THE PAINT-BRUSH was beautifully loaded, fat with white gloss but not dripping, when the telephone rang. Lydia cursed.

It had been mid-morning before she'd got down to what she thought of as proper work. The first two hours had been spent in returning the "dining-room" to a bare-board state in which she could work at it, and this she'd done grudgingly, with an unusual sense of resentment that Richard should get out of it by going off to his crammers, and another layer of resentment that she'd let herself in for entertaining according to the mores of a life-style which she detested. During her coffee-break she had sat sniffing the odourless steam and wondering whether she was getting flu, or had eaten a dubious mussel, or was enduring for the first time in her life a real hangover. Just to suggest these possibilities was to dismiss them, and at the same time to force herself to admit that her bile and spleen were caused by Lalage. The physical symptoms—dusty tongue, half headache, dreariness in the blood—were the result of a bad night's sleep, itself the result of undigested fury. The mental symptom was self-disgust, trying to masquerade as self-righteousness.

So, though there was still plenty of clearing-up to be done she had settled down after her coffee-break to a job she normally enjoyed, laying a smoothly professional layer of gloss paint onto a skirtingboard. It was going well—paint just the right thickness, brush not losing any hairs, her own hand steady and precise—when the telephone rang. I know who that is, she thought. She was right.

"I'm sorry," said the husky but childish voice.

For the moment Lydia was unable to speak.

"Is that you, Liz?"

"Yes."

"I'm sorry. I really am. I behaved unspeakably."

"It doesn't matter."

"Yes it does. Honestly, I just couldn't help myself."

"I know."

"You're a saint. *You* don't go about behaving unspeakably because you can't help yourself."

"Yes I do. I can't help myself . . . if you were here, I'd hit you, hard."

"Oh, darling! But . . ."

"Forget it. It's all ancient history."

"I didn't realise that you . . ."

"Now listen. I'm not cross with you. I'm furious."

"But . . ."

"Shut up! I'm not cross with you for hitting it off with Paul, because that's what I wanted, roughly. I'm not cross with you for spoiling the party, because you didn't, it was OK after you left, and anyway that sort of party is stupid. But I am furious with you because I can't help it. That's all. Thank you for ringing. You've left your dress and your car behind. I'll be in this evening if you want to come and pick them up."

"Hang on. There's two other things."

"Yes?"

"You probably won't be very pleased about this either, but I felt so awful that I've bought you a tree."

"A *what*?"

"It isn't a very big one—I mean it won't grow into a spreading oak or anything. It's very pretty. I saw one in a friend's garden and it has delicious little whitey-pink flowers most of the winter. Prunus subhirtella autumnalis. I thought you might put it where the roses came out, and pavement underneath . . . Liz, I'll cancel it if you don't want it. I just thought . . ."

"No, it's all right. I mean, thanks, darling, that'll be lovely, it's just what I wanted. I expect. I didn't know what to do with that bit, so it's nice to have my mind made up for me."

"Oh, super! You wouldn't like two? I mean, a pair? I mean . . . oh, pull yourself together, woman! I've been so worried. I didn't know what to *say*."

"Say it with trees."

"Oh, Liz, you are a saint! Shall I order another one?"

"One will be masses, thanks. What was the other thing? I've got a wet paint-brush."

"Oh, I'm sorry . . . I didn't know . . . yes, of course I did, because there's always something like that. Er, it's about Paul, I'm afraid."

"Yes."

"What do you know about him?"

"He's my new tenant. He's a Livonian exile, and now he's Minister of Maritime Affairs in the Government. He's got his own ship, and he seems to be pretty rich. But he likes to do things for himself. He's very efficient with his hands."

Lalage giggled.

"Anything else?" hissed Lydia.

"Oh, God, I *am* putting my foot in it. I haven't fallen for anyone that way for absolute years. Him too, I think. We're the same kind of animal. Usually I like to see my blokes crawl a bit, sometimes . . . but . . . I suppose it's because we're both utterly selfish, so at least we've got that to respect each other for . . . you can be honest with somebody like that . . ."

"Dickie adores him," said Lydia. She knew there was no point in setting up prickly zarebas of anger and envy—they'd only have to come down again.

"That's what I wanted to ask you about," said Lalage, surprisingly. "Not just Dickie—all of you. Did you know Paul's absolutely obsessed by you? I don't mean just you, Liz, as a potential mark, I mean the set-up. He's like an anthropologist who wants to know all about a tribe."

"What did you tell him?" It looked as though the zarebas were going to have to go up after all.

"I told him to mind his own business. I was pretty shirty at first, because I thought it meant he'd only fallen for me because he couldn't have you—I mean, someone like that you're a sort of challenge to, aren't you? Then I saw it wasn't that, so I told him things anyone could find out, like Dad being a surgeon and marrying twice, and Richard having been in the army, and you being a bit of a left-wing nut. I let him look over the hedge, but I didn't ask him into your garden."

"I expect that's all right."

"Yes, but . . ."

"Well?"

"Look, Liz, this is pure hunch. But there's something going on."

"What on earth do you mean?"

"I don't know."

"What kind of something, Lal? Do you mean he's using

104

his ship to smuggle heroin, or something like that?"

"I don't think so. I don't think you're in it, though. I'm not even sure he is. Of course as soon as I got to the office I started to find out all I could about him. His ship's OK, and he's set up a nice steady two-way series of contracts between London and Helsinki. There's enough loot there to support his life-style. But . . . look, he's not really the same sort as your old men in your Government, is he? What's he doing there?"

"He's a Liv. The Russians chucked a lot of people out. They don't all have to be the same as each other."

"I know, but . . . one idea I had was he might be involved in some sort of currency juggling, using your old men as a front. I can't quite see how it would work, if it's roubles—there's no profit in getting roubles out, only getting dollars in, and then the profit's in Russia—perhaps it's something to do with old Czarist bonds, or there might be an unredeemed Livonian loan or something. Would you mind, Liz?"

"Mind? Oh, I see. I don't really want my old men taken for a ride, but otherwise I'm all for it. The more rats there are in the capitalist system, the sooner it'll fall apart."

"Squeak, squeak."

"Any rats that get fat will be collected and cooked by recipes in the Little Red Cookbook."

"I think you're marvelous, darling. Do take care. I don't believe in much except my own comfort, but while you and Richard are OK I know there are higher things in life. Bye, darling."

Lydia went back to her painting. She was glad Lalage had called, not because it had really settled anything but because her own fury had somehow unknotted itself during the last few minutes and ravelled smoothly away to nothing. At least I haven't got rats, she thought. Only rots which, checked in one place, could still put out creeping grey strands, invisible behind paper and plaster, to reach and infect fresh timber, so that all the work had to be done again. That's what the world's really like, she thought. Rats? Rats!

—. .—. .— —. .— snickered the key. Lydia lifted down from the shelf the stopwatch she had used for rallying before she ever met Richard. Dickie crouched in the corner behind a pile of cardboard boxes, waiting for the answer to his call sign.

After a brief pause the metallic note beeped .— —. . . .— three times. She pressed the starter knob. Paul had recorded quite a long message and seemed to be going slightly faster; trying to read the letters in her head she got lost almost at once, so she returned to modifying the back suspension of her dream car. When the Morse ended she pressed the stop button and slid her sketches under the armchair. From the hiding-place a pigeon crooned.

"All clear," said Lydia. "A patrol came past five minutes ago. I gave the corporal a slice of fruit cake."

Dickie's head poked up like a gopher's from its burrow. He even sniffed the air for danger. Then on tip-toe he crept across the room and slid a sheet of paper onto Lydia's lap. The lines of dots and dashes were far neater than any writing he had ever done.

"Couldn't you write the letters underneath, darling?" coaxed Lydia. "I'm only an ignorant cobbler's wife. You can't expect me to read Morse."

"I'll read it," he whispered. His lips puckered to shape each letter but he didn't say them aloud until he had wrestled a word clear.

"Ammo ... train ... at ... pass ... 0300 ... what's huh rrr sss?"

"Hours. It's a short way of spelling it. That means three o'clock in the morning. I'll be in bed, fast asleep."

"I'll be up in the pass with Aaku, of course."

He picked his way through the message, making three mistakes and twice needing help with words that didn't pronounce themselves easily—Dickie was receiving at just under five words a minute now, when a month before he had been taking a sulky minute to drag one word out of ordinary letters. The Morse Code, by reaching his mind through his ear, had somehow by-passed whatever was causing the blockage between mind and eye. Even the dots and dashes on the paper were representations of sounds, and he seemed able to use them because of that. The next stage was to persuade him that letters were really much the same.

Lydia, miming secrecy and caution, fetched from its hiding-place behind the bookshelf an old fountain pen.

"Number Eight brought that this morning," she said.

Forgetting to go to his secret radio Dickie lay on the floor, unscrewing the cap of the pen and teased out the cylinder of paper that Lydia had hidden there. He was painfully turning the letters into dots and dashes when the phone rang.

"May I speak to Lady Timms?"

"That's me."

"Ah, good. This is Diarghi, from the Russian Embassy. How are you?"

"Fine, thanks. You never sent me those references. I was beginning to wonder . . ."

"Exactly. Well, I have an apology to make. Baltic affairs are not my subject, and I'm afraid I relied too much on memory. When I came to check the references, I discovered that I'd made a mistake. What I told you about Busch is approximately correct, but I'd confused Linden with another man."

"Oh! Are you sure?"

"Yes, why?"

"Well, our Central Library has a run of Hansards, and when I was taking some books back I thought I'd see if I couldn't find something, and I did."

"It was the same name, and he was a minister in the Livonian Government in exile."

"Of course, of course—that is how I came to make the mistake. I have since consulted our specialist on the area, and I find that the Lindens are a large clan. Naturally, after the publicity, the man I was telling you about faded into the background. I believe he died in Canada."

"I see. Well, thank you for letting me know. I wasn't going to do anything about it, as a matter of fact."

There was a pause. Dickie's key beeped his call-sign. Mr Diarghi coughed.

."We have a crossed line, I think," he said.

"What? No. No that's OK. It's just my son using a Morse key."

"Ah."

No wonder he sounded relieved. It's bad enough having to ring up British citizens and tell them that you've been feeding them mistaken propaganda, but the sudden intrusion of a burst of amateur Morse into your conversation must produce a real chill of alarm.

"Well, there it is," he said rather abruptly. "I hope my misinformation hasn't caused you any distress. I'd very much like to meet you again when I have made further progress with my report."

A few polite half-promises on both sides, and he rang off.

The Morse key beeped on. Lydia blessed Paul in her heart. It was a typically male piece of behavior to devise such a fully-functioning toy, and to explain in total seriousness that a real spy can't expect to have his messages answered at once, supposing they get through at all. Upstairs the patient tape, triggered by the call sign, would be taking down Lydia's contribution to the bloody farce of this imaginary war, and quite soon Richard would come home and play the part of the stupid Russian police, angrily searching the basement and shouting threats and commands, but never, somehow, finding the secret hide-out.

20

"ALL RIGHT," said Lydia, "I'll get a taxi. It's as urgent as that?"

"Yes," said Richard's voice, very strained.

"OK, I'll come at once."

"Trouble?" asked Lalage as she put down the receiver.

"Yes, I don't know what. Can I leave Dickie here? I'll ring you up when I've sorted things out."

"Lovely—it doesn't matter how long. There's a stack of food and Dad's longing to read him *Greenmantle* . . . Oh, hell! Dad's got some gen for you about a corpse or something."

"Bother. That'll have to wait. With any luck I'll be back in a couple of hours."

"No hurry. I was going out with Paul, but he'll be quite happy to stay here and play war-games with the other fellows, God rot their masculine guts. Sure you don't want me to come with you?"

"No thanks. See you."

She was in luck. A taxi was putting down a very shaky old man two doors along the street, so when the fumbling fingers had at last counted out the tiny tip she was able to jump in, sit back on the tatty mock leather, and fret. What the hell could be happening at Devon Crescent that Richard needed her to cope with, and that he couldn't explain on the telephone? He sounded as though there'd been someone in the room with him, too. Was it some blood-curdling quarrel between tenants? Had Don Pumice come home half-crazed? Had the joists under the Government's store room given way? And killed Paul Vaklins? That would account for Richard's reticence, if he'd known Lalage might be listening. If that floor had collapsed, what about the one below? If Mrs Pumice were in, and baby Trevor, and the Evanses on the floor below that, each fall adding its weight and impact . . .

The streets were all sleepy with Sunday, and the taxi buzzed rapidly through like a bluebottle in an empty kitchen. As it swung into Devon Crescent the curve of the buildings hid Number Eleven, but Lydia crouched forward with the fare and tip hot in her palm, straining to see what columns of smoke or dust were streaming from which smashed windows. Then, when her house came into view, she saw the whole façade was as calm as a tomb.

Nearer, she saw that something was up. A small crowd was gathered round her gate, and several loiterers stood on the opposite pavement, staring. The taxi drew up behind a double-parked car, but she didn't notice that it was a police car until she'd paid her fare. A uniformed constable stopped her at the front gate.

"Keep back, *if* you please," he said.

"I live here. This is my house."

"If you'll have a word with the officer at the front door there. Him in the grey hat."

Drugs? Stan Pelletier back from university with pockets full of pot? Or Mrs Pumice—she'd come very suddenly into a windfall. Or the Government in some crooked deal, as Lalage had hinted? Again that might account for Richard . . .

The policeman at the door gave her no clue. He simply nodded and led her into Mrs Pelletier's back room, dark with the enormous pieces of mahogany furniture that had come with the house. Richard was there, very grey and twitchy, sitting on the edge of the big bed. Lydia ran across to him.

"Are you all right, darling? What's up?"

He looked up, made an effort and knew her. He smiled.

"Ah, you made it. That was quick."

"What's going on darling? Please!"

He shook his head. Somebody coughed. Lydia swung round and saw a tall, glossily tanned young man with curly hair and long side-burns.

"Gentleman's a bit shook up, I'm afraid, ma'am. The Superintendent won't be long now, I expect."

"I must know what's going on. Where is he?"

"Now, ma'am . . ."

"Are you seriously going to try to stop me going where I like in my own house? You haven't any authority to do so. In fact, as far as I'm concerned you haven't any authority to be here at all. Now, where is this Superintendent?"

The man's tan didn't actually pale, but it lost some of its

110

lustre. He was hesitating about standing out of her way when Lydia heard voices and footsteps coming up the back stairs from the basement or the garden door. The policeman coughed again, reclothed himself in authority with the surreptitious speed of a man tucking his shirttail into his trousers in a public place, and opened the door.

A slim, dreary-looking man entered, grey haired, grey-lipped, solemn as a verger. Behind him came a much bigger man with a round, red, shiny face; he looked like a bather in a Donald McGill postcard.

"Are you the Superintendent?" said Lydia.

"Superintendent Austen, CID," said the grey man. "This is Sergeant Eissmann. You are, er, Lady Timms?"

"That's right. Now, could you please tell me what's going on?"

He didn't answer but crossed to the window.

"If you'd come here a moment, Lady Timms," he said.

Lydia hesitated, then joined him. The garden had changed. When Lydia had left it after lunch it had been a stodgy rectangle of raked earth, crossed in one place by the paved path and in another by the planks the spy had put down so that Mrs Pelletier could reach her washing-line. Now there were a lot more planks, a huge mound of earth, and four or five men standing about. One of them was kneeling down just beyond the mound and another was taking photographs of something there. Further away two more seemed to be laying out a sort of tent.

"What the hell's going on?" said Lydia.

"Now, madam," said Superintendent Austen in the voice of a shop-walker trying to soothe a fierce customer, "can you tell me exactly when that patch of earth out there was last dug over? It appears to be quite recently."

"Why? What's happened?"

"We'll come to that later. I asked you . . ."

"We'll come to it now. What's happening? Why are you here?"

"If you please, madam . . ."

"Unless you give me a reasonable explanation of your presence I shall ask you to leave my house."

Richard groaned. Lydia went and sat beside him and gripped his limp hand.

"It's all right, darling," she said gently. "There's no reason why I should tell him anything until he's satisfied me that he's got some sort of right to know."

Sergeant Eissmann sucked in his breath.

"Sir Richard asked us to come," said Superintendent Austen. His tone of voice hadn't altered, but two little bunches of muscle had appeared just below his cheek-bones.

"That's all right," said Lydia, taking care not to snap at him because she didn't want to upset Richard any more. "But as you can see my husband is in a state of shock, and I need to know why. In fact the garden was thoroughly dug over the Monday before last, a fortnight ago. Now will you tell me what's happening?"

"A fortnight ago," said the Superintendent in a musing voice. Sergeant Eissmann had a notebook out and wrote a few words. Lydia discovered that she was squeezing Richard's hand so hard that she must be hurting him. She willed herself calm.

"Superintendent," she said, "whatever you're doing you're doing it in a very stupid way, exactly calculated to get minimum help from me."

"I am conducting an investigation into what looks like a case of murder," said the Superintendent.

"Murder! Who?"

"I dug up a hand," whispered Richard. "It came out of the clay. It was like a fungus."

(That wasn't so bad, if he could talk about it. For the first time since she'd come into the room Lydia felt that she could relax her protection slightly. But . . . a hand!)

"We do not yet know who," said the Superintendent. "An elderly woman. My men have only just finished clearing the earth from the body."

"Do you want me to see if I know her?" said Lydia. "Is she . . . recognisable?"

"Not so bad," said Sergeant Eissmann, beaming. "I've seen much worse."

"I was planting the tree," whispered Richard. Lydia squeezed his hand again and stood up.

"I won't be long, darling," she said.

"An identification would certainly be of value," said Superintendent Austen, "but I would prefer . . ."

"Let's get it over," said Lydia. "Can somebody please stay with my husband?"

"You take her down, Dave," said the Superintendent.

Sergeant Eissmann hummed a dreary humn-tune as he followed her down the stairs to the basement. As she was opening the garden door he said, "If I was you ma'am, I'd ease up on the super a bit. You won't get much change out of him, whatever you say."

Lydia smiled tightly at him. She realised now that it was her antipathy to the Superintendent that had trapped her into marching off like this to peer into the eyes of death. She began to feel very withdrawn into herself, very screwed-up. Outside she discovered that, although there was plenty of daylight left, the air seemed drab, as if it were already dusk. A chill came out of the darkening sky, a chill rose from the raw earth. Sergeant Eissmann's hand steadied her across the boards and round the neat-piled mound. Lalage's tree, its roots still wrapped in sacking, lay to one side.

Just beyond the mound was a rectangular hole. The photographer had fixed a floodlight to shine on its lip, and his assistant was adjusting a white cardboard arrow to point at something under its glare.

"Borrow your light a mo so that the lady can see what's what?" said Sergeant Eissmann.

"Jesus Christ, how d'you expect me . . ." muttered the photographer, but he swung the lamp over and made it glare down into the hole. Lydia stepped forward on the greasy plank.

The woman lay there, wrapped in a curious tube of coarse raw cotton or cheap canvas; it was torn on one side where Richard's spade had sliced down; a bony hand showed. Somebody had cut the top end of the tube with greater care and folded the flaps back to make a sort of high-winged collar through which the head poked out. The cheeks and forehead were streaked with yellow clay and the sparse hair was full of the stuff. Between the streaks the flesh seemed bruised and wrinkled, like a fungus as Richard had said, or like the hand of a child who has stayed too long in the bath. The eyes, mercifully, were closed, but the mouth below the bony little nose hung open in an everlasting snore. The woman looked diseased, leprous under the fierce light, but there was no mistaking her.

"It's Mrs Newbury!" Lydia gasped. "But we buried her! Weeks ago! Why did you plant it there? She got out of her box! You said she would! Getting out and coming for him! Getting out and coming for him!"

Her voice was no longer her own but an animal shriek. The laughter followed it, rising up her throat like vomit. Each hooting gasp seemed to end in a muscular contraction which could only be released by another series of shrieks. Inside

113

this ghastly, melodramatic creature the real Lydia waited, appalled, unable to interfere. She was quite conscious of how Sergeant Eissmann took the creature by the elbow and led it away across the planks and into a dark place, and there was Richard coming down the stairs to hold her close while the shrieking creature appeased itself and the fit died out in shudders and whimpers.

"I'm sorry," she mumbled. "I don't know why I did that. I'm all right now."

"That bloody man," said Richard. "He shouldn't have let you ..."

Her lungs sucked in breath for a new bout of hysteria, but she clenched her teeth and hands and willed her body into decency.

"It must have been worse for you, darling," she said.

"I'm getting over it, I think. Can you tackle the stairs?"

They were still holding hands like lovers in a tulip garden when they reached the Pelletiers' back room. Superintendent Austen looked no different, as uninterested in what had happened as if Lydia had merely left the room to put on a kettle for coffee. But Sergeant Eissmann fetched her a chair.

"Now," said the Superintendent, "I believe that you can clear up the identification."

"It's Mrs Newbury," said Lydia.

"No!" said Richard.

"Please, sir," said the Superintendent. "Yes, madam?"

"She was one of my tenants. She died of a fall in her room at the end of January. I went to the inquest and then to the funeral, at Kensal Green. We buried her. I tell you, we buried her!"

"Take it easy, madam. We will go into that later. You are quite certain of this identification?"

"Yes. In fact Mrs Pumice has got a photograph of her. She lives on the second floor, left-hand side as you come up the stairs."

"Dave," said the Superintendent. Sergeant Eissmann rose and left.

"Now, I'd like to return to the question of when the garden was dug, and why, and by whom. A fortnight ago, you say?"

"That's right. I and several of my neighbours employ a casual labourer called Mr Roberts to do our gardens. It was a complete mess, with only a few scrubby old roses, so I asked him to dig it right through."

"What do you mean when you say it was a mess?"

114

"Oh, I've been doing a lot of repairs to the house, and throwing out timber and things, and burning everything I could. But in fact it hadn't been a *garden* for several years."

"So you mightn't have noticed if somebody had buried the body in there earlier?"

Lydia rose and walked to the window. The photographer and his helpers were still mopping and mowing around the grave like students of the black arts.

"Oh yes, I think I would," she said. "That bit was usually fairly clear. But surely you can tell by the state of the soil whether the grave was dug before or after Mr Roberts worked it over."

"That's as may be," said the Superintendent. Lydia felt her antipathy rising again—he seemed to be just the sort of official she most detested, giving nothing, secretive for secrecy's sake, a servant of the system, indifferent to the individual people whom the system chumbled about. Sergeant Eissmann came back looking cheerier than ever and gave him the newspaper cutting. The Superintendent gazed at it, rubbing his chin.

"Take a dekko at the caption," said Sergeant Eissmann.

At once the Superintendent's eyebrows rose and his lips pursed into a soundless, prurient whistle.

"Do you know if the deceased was the mother of a woman called Procne Newbury?" he asked.

"That's right," said Lydia, grudgingly.

"We've got one reporter here already," said Sergeant Eissmann. "I guess we'll have the lot along in half an hour."

"Can't be helped," said the Superintendent, looking not at all displeased. "Now, madam, refresh my memory. You say this Mrs Newbury died longer ago than the Monday before last."

Carefully, picking her words so that she herself gave nothing away either, Lydia went through the story from the discovery of Mrs Newbury dead in her room until her funeral.

"So you identified her for the coroner's court?" said the Superintendent at one point.

"That's right."

"Well, now, I don't want to distress you, but can you remember whether her skin was then in a normal condition?"

"Normal?"

"You must have seen that the skin is now in a very peculiar state, wrinkled and . . ."

"Don't go on! No, it was quite normal. A bit pale. She

115

always had rather a flushed complexion when she was alive, but that may have been because she was usually het up about something. There was a bit of blood and a bruise on her temple. I thought that . . . out there . . . that was just being in the ground . . ."

The Superintendent shook his head, keeping to himself yet another secret not to be revealed to the common herd. Lydia went on.

"I see," he said when she'd finished. "Now is there any possibility of Mrs Newbury having had a twin sister?"

"Not that I know of. In fact she once told me that she was an only child."

"Can you tell me the circumstances of that conversation?"

"It isn't relevant."

"Allow me to judge that."

"No, thanks."

Lydia felt that there was no reason why she should recount the whole history of Mrs Newbury's long campaign to persuade her to have a few brothers and sisters for Dickie. He stared at her, glanced at Sergeant Eissmann's notebook and shrugged.

"Well then, can you let me know the name and address of the undertakers responsible for the funeral at Kensal Green?"

"I'm afraid not. I don't know. The Government arranged all that."

"The Government!"

"I'm sorry. The top two floors of this house are let to the Livonian Consulate. Livonia used to be the smallest of the Baltic republics before the Russians took over, and this is really the Livonian Government in Exile. We call them the Government. Mrs Newbury was their cleaner and they arranged rather a grand funeral for her . . . they'll be very put out about this. Oh, dear. Sunday. Mr Obb has a flat up there, and he was the one who fixed it. He might . . ."

"By the way, they've got diplomatic immunity," said Richard in a perfectly normal voice. Lydia almost laughed aloud with pleasure and relief to hear him talking like that, and making such a typically Richardy point, too. It had the effect of tilting Lydia's world back onto its proper axis; what had happened ceased to be nightmare and became a real event, sudden and horrible but copable-with. Priorities emerged.

"When can you move the body?" she said. "I don't want to bring our son home till it's gone."

The Superintendent ignored her. Back out of the nightmare Lydia perceived now that he was a man who had reached that crucial level in the hierarchy where he could cope with his own job, but only just. Faced with immune diplomats and twice-buried but unmurdered bodies of the mothers of famous harlots and small boys needing to come home, his mind slid away to areas he understood.

"Just go and see whether we've got any reporters, Dave," he said.

"OK, OK," said Sergeant Eissmann.

"Would you like me to take you up and introduce you to Mr Obb, if he's there?" said Richard. "I've been a diplomat, so I know the ropes."

Typically, Superintendent Austen accepted the suggestion almost with eagerness, because it came from a man. While they were out of the room Lydia telephoned Lalage, told her what had happened, and asked her to bring Dickie round in an hour. As soon as she put the receiver down the phone rang again. It was a reporter from the *Sun*, asking her to confirm the news. She cut him off without answering. The machine rang again, and this time she simply left the receiver off. Within five minutes somebody had persuaded the engineers to start the howler. Lydia unscrewed the earpiece and slid the diaphragm clear—she reckoned that it would need a lot of influence to get an engineer out to Devon Crescent on a Sunday evening, and at least the police could deal with any reporters who came to the door.

A bit later Superintendent Austen came down again, to ask for the key to what was now Paul Vaklin's room. Lydia refused to let him have it without Paul's permission. That meant reassembling the phone and ringing up Lalage again. Paul was there and said he'd come straight round. That in turn meant another fight with Austen about whether the body could now be taken away, so that Paul could bring Dickie with him. Austen was still refusing when Sergeant Eissmann came in to say that the job had already been done, and did the Superintendent want to be present at the autopsy. Without waiting for permission, Lydia fixed up with Paul and dismantled the phone again. By the time she'd done that the policemen were going out of the door.

"By the way," she called, "Mr Roberts—the gardener—will be here to-morrow morning. Do you want to see him?"

"Instructions will be left with the officer on duty at the door," snapped the Superintendent, and stalked away, the model of petty dignity.

Lydia smiled to herself as she poured water into the kettle.

"I think you might give him a bit more rope, darling," said Richard. His voice sounded tired but normal.

"Are you all right, darling?" she said.

"I'm fine. It was a shock, and I thought I was cracking up again, but then you turned up, and that was better, and as soon as you said it was Mrs Newbury that was all right."

"Why on earth . . ."

"Not knowing was what hit me."

"But we buried her!"

"You buried somebody else. The Government had the coffin brought home, and all that rigmarole, because they'd got somebody else to bury. Or possibly something else—documents, gold—no, that would be too heavy—oh, it doesn't matter. Now it's their look-out."

"I wonder if you're right. How did you get on with them?"

"It was Obb—very polite, very concerned, very stiff. Not saying anything. Oh, yes, we got the undertaker's name out of him, that's all. Poor old Austen, with Obb giving him the brush-off upstairs and you kicking him in the teeth down here. Do go a bit easy on him, darling."

"But . . ."

"What's the point? He'll get what he wants in the end, and you only make an enemy of him."

"OK, I'll try to be polite, but . . . I mean, Paul's key! He simply wasn't entitled to it. I *couldn't* have given it to him!"

"I suppose so. What's for supper? Shall I peel the spuds?"

Ten minutes later Lalage brought Dickie down to the basement. He was in a state of frenzied thrill at the presence of so many policemen, and though Lydia had drawn the curtains he somehow managed to spot the tent that now covered the hole in the garden. Richard told him firmly that it was all a secret, and he spent the hour till his bed-time sending a long message about it up to Paul. No answer came.

21

She told Dickie next morning, as she was walking with him to his play-group—it was holidays now, but half-a-dozen mums worked a rota system with their kids. There had still been a policeman on the door, and one or two loiterers, and a depressed man taking photographs of anybody who went in or out.

"Why's he doing that?" asked Dickie. "Are we famous?"

"Not yet, thank heavens," said Lydia. "Do you remember Mrs Newbury?"

"She's dead."

"That's right. Well, there seems to have been a mistake about her funeral. I don't know how it happened, but she got buried in our garden, instead of in the cemetery, and the police want to find out why. That's all."

"But the man took a picture of *us*."

"Well, you see, this sort of mistake doesn't happen very often—in fact it's very rare—so I suppose some people might think it's interesting enough to put in a newspaper."

"Will there be a picture of us?"

"I don't think so. They always take far more pictures than they can possibly use, just in case."

"Like a football. Derek's father does that. He takes hundreds of pictures, and only sometimes it's a goal."

"Yes, just like that."

And that was that. All over. No fuss, no spores to float through the darkness inside his little skull, settle in some recess and grow slowly into nightmare. Children have a marvellous ability to treat everything that happens as if it were normal. On her way back to Devon Crescent Lydia determined to do the same herself. To-day would be an ordinary day. She planned to wallpaper the back room and she'd do just that. Great. April began to sparkle along the roof-tops, to glisten in the gutters, to twinkle from passing cars. Her own sudden cheerfulness seemed to bounce like the sunlight off people and objects. The policeman at the door grinned at her as she passed.

"Have you seen Mr Roberts, that's the gardener?" she said.

"No ma'am. The super's been asking for him too."

"Bother. Perhaps he's decided to do a turn at one of the other houses. If anyone wants me I'll be downstairs, in the back room."

"Very good."

She mixed Polycell, got the trestle out, fetched the steps and her big scissors and measured and cut the first strip. She was slithering paste onto it when she heard men's voices, and feet on the bare stairs. To-day is an ordinary day, she told herself. I'll be patient with the bastards.

"Good morning, Superintendent," she said, still slapping away with the brush. "Do you want me?"

"If you can spare the time, madam."

"That's all right, provided you don't mind if I go on working. You'll find a couple of chairs in the kitchen, Sergeant, if you'd like to sit down. I'm afraid Mr Roberts hasn't turned up."

"So I am told," said Austen, in a dry voice.

"He's a bit of a hermit. Perhaps he was frightened off by the people at the gate. It might be worth seeing whether he's gone to any of the other gardens instead."

She rattled off the numbers of the relevant houses. Sergeant Eissmann left to instruct some underling and Austen himself fetched the chairs. Lydia folded the bottom third of her paper up on itself, picked up the two top corners and climbed the steps by the wall. Her plumb-line hung tremorless against the mottled plaster. The sergeant came back as she was easing the top eighteen inches smooth.

"It's all right," she said. "I can talk while I'm doing this."

"Wish I had a wife or two like you," said Sergeant Eissmann.

"Now, madam," said Austen, "first I want to check a detail about the funeral. The undertaker tells me that when he brought the coffin back here on the night of the fifth of February the room was prepared for some kind of wake. Is that correct?"

"Yes. It wasn't exactly a wake. I told you that Mrs Newbury did the cleaning for the Livonian Consulate. She'd done it for a long time. Mr Obb told me that they wanted to bury her properly—rather grandly, in fact—to show their

120

appreciation. One of their national customs is that they sit up with the body all night before the funeral."

"I see. Did you go into the room while the coffin was there?"

Satisfied with the hang of her paper Lydia peeled the bottom section down and began to ease the wrinkles out to the sides.

"I showed the men where to put it when they came," she said. "But after that . . . I don't even know whether the Livs did watch all night—it's just that Mr Obb said they would."

"I see. Now, madam, the body was buried approximately three feet down. If your husband had not started to dig a hole for the tree there it wouldn't have been found, being below the normal level of cultivation. The question is, who knew that he would plant the tree just there? Have you mentioned this to anyone?"

"No," said Lydia, easing the top of her strip clear so that she could cut it true to the ceiling. "Nobody knew. We hadn't actually decided. I rather thought I'd like it in the middle, where the rosebed had been, but he thought that would darken this window too much. I left it to him when I went out."

"Was that what you were referring to when you said 'Why did you plant it there?' "

"Did I? When did I say that?"

She had the top of the paper fitted now and began to come down the steps, feeling curiously shivery.

"When you were by the hole, madam. Apparently you said, or rather shouted, 'Why did you plant it there?' Also something about coming out of a box."

"It's Mrs Newbury," said Sergeant Eissmann, reading from his notebook in a drab, heavy voice. "But we buried her. Weeks ago. Why did you plant it there? She got out of her box. You said she would. Getting out and coming for him (twice)."

It seemed lucky that she had reached the bottom of the steps, and there they were, to sit on, carefully, feeling for them in case she collapsed in the suddenly darkened room. She put her head in her hands.

"Did I say that? I don't remember. Sorry."

"Take it easy," said Sergeant Eissmann.

"I'm sorry, I really don't remember anything that happened out there, except that I recognised Mrs Newbury and then I had hysterics. Read it again."

121

"Have a smoke first?" suggested the Sergeant.

As she reached gratefully for the packet she saw Austen's eyes gazing at her with intense, withdrawn interest. Eissmann was smiling, but his eyes had the same look. Eissmann, nice man, she thought as she lit up. Austen, nasty man. The usual team. Bastards. Anger steadied her, so that she could listen without emotion to the words she was supposed to have spoken.

"Yes, I see," she said. "The bit about where my husband planted the tree is obvious. The other part is all to do with a conversation we had the day they brought the body back. You're supposed to let small children acquire some experience of death, and I discussed with my husband whether I shouldn't take Dickie into the room where the coffin was. He quite rightfully told me it was a bad idea, as Dickie used to be rather afraid of Mrs Newbury, so he might have nightmares about her getting out of the box and coming for him."

She looked up. Eissmann was still smiling his trained smile, but there was a new expression on Austen's face.

"You seriously mean to tell me," he said, "that you were proposing to take a kiddie into a room with a coffin in it, to let him look?"

Voice and feature were those one might see on the face of a respectable Borough Councillor who has just been told that some blue film is a superlative expression of artistic freedom.

"We only talked about it," said Lydia. "Whether I would have done it is my own affair. It only concerns you because it explains what you say I said in the garden."

Austen resumed his clinical mask with a speed that reminded Lydia of her father. He paused to let Eissmann finish taking a note of what she'd said. Lydia found herself irritated by this process, an irrational disgust caused partly by Austen's own persona and partly by dislike at having her words taken down and filed away—particularly words screamed involuntarily by that other Lydia who usually slept the days away in secret and only stirred about once a month to drift and then scramble through a nightmare. To ease her tension she got off the steps and marked and trimmed the lower end of her strip. She was smoothing it back when Austen coughed for her attention.

"Now," he said in a back-to-business voice, "may I ask

122

you to look at a few photographs for us? We want to see whether you can identify a man."

"Of course."

"I must warn you that the man is dead."

"Oh."

"Tisn't that horrible," said Eissmann. "A bit peculiar, only, but not bloody or anything."

"OK. Will this take long? I do want to get the papering done before my son comes back. He's an absolute devil with glue."

"If you'll look at the pictures I don't think we'll need to bother you again for a while."

"OK." Lydia took an uncomforting suck at her fag and stubbed it out.

The prints were large and shiny. At first Lydia thought that she was looking at a bit of mildly experimental portrait sculpture, then she saw that the thing was not puddled plaster but flesh. It was a sunken-cheeked, bald old man. His eyes were shut. His ears were large, thin and very protruding, his mouth wide and sharply turned down at the corners. You could imagine him sitting on a park bench, wearing a shabby overcoat and leaning forward over his walking-stick, trying to suck the sunlight into his veins to enrich the thin, sad blood. Only if you had seen him sitting like that you would have immediately looked away, rather than stare at the strange ailment that affected all his skin, innumerable seams and puckering which did not follow the natural creaselines that one sometimes sees on old men's faces, but wandered and crossed at random.

"It's the same as Mrs Newbury!" she said.

"Only he'd been in it longer," said Sergeant Eissmann.

"In what?"

The Superintendent managed to look as though he alone knew. The Sergeant simply shrugged.

"Some kind of alcohol," he said. "The lab say he's never going to rot now, he's been soaking in it that long."

Lydia looked at the other photographs. Some were in profile and two showed the whole body, naked and unwounded, but all pocked and puddled with the same patterning as the face.

"How tall was he?" she asked.

"Little fellow," said the Sergeant. "They'd put in a couple of polythene bags, full of sand, to bring it up to the weight when the old lady was in it."

"I'm afraid I've never seen him before," said Lydia. "You mean they buried him instead of Mrs Newbury?"

"Seems so," said the Sergeant.

Lydia gazed steadily at the long-imagined, but (now she saw it) totally strange face. What had brought him to this end?

"Was he . . . I mean, did he die naturally?" she asked.

"Cancer of the liver," said the Sergeant. "Rather him than me."

"Now, let's get this straight," said the Superintendent. "You say you have no idea who this man was, nor how he came to be buried instead of Mrs Newbury?"

Lydia hated lying, but her antipathy to him let her do so now almost with pleasure.

"No," she said, briskly. "Is that all?"

"That's all . . . for the moment," he answered. He managed to load the pause with reservations, but Sergeant Eissmann winked as they left. At last their footsteps faded.

Lydia measured and hung a second strip of paper before she allowed herself to think about the interview, and then the image on the top of her mind turned out to be that of the strangely wrinkled corpse of a little old man, buried in secret so far from home. Aaku Aakisen, leader of the Livonian Resistance. Little Aaku with his sticky-out ears. *We had an old man, a servant, who made excellent varosh, very skilled, very careful. But then he died* . . . What do you do, when all the time he's supposed to be attracting propaganda values to your cause by living on in the icy, licy hell of Siberia? Obviously, you preserve his body by popping it into a barrel of strong alcohol. There it stays . . . how long? Years. Then (for the random mercy of God sends an occasional blessing even to the forgotten Livs) Mrs Newbury dies, and the opportunity arises to give the national hero a grand burial, if under an assumed name and sex, but better than lying soaking in *varosh*. Mrs Newbury takes up that sinister duty. Yes, they'd needed to pack the coffin with a couple of sandbags to make up the extra weight, which meant, presumably, that there had been extra volume also. Mrs Newbury had displaced more *varosh* than old Aaku, so the liquor had overflowed, run down between the floorboards and made a strange sticky patch on the ceiling below. Lydia had actually stretched out her hand towards the very bin . . . *Not to touch, please! Varosh is most infectable!* Ugh. Yes, Mrs Newbury had still been huddled in there, in the amniotic booze, because it had been days later when Lydia had stood in the garden with the spy and seen Count Linden staring down at that convenient patch of fresh-dug earth in which Mrs Newbury could be buried hugger-mugger. When? Why, the night of the Russian Embassy reception, because the only way out to the garden was through the basement, which meant that the Timmses had to be out of the way. So Paul knew. Of course he did. In the car, going to the cemetery, Lydia had mentioned Aakisen out of the blue and Paul had been startled. Then, very quickly, he had come up with the plausible pretence that she'd thought that the Livs were burying Aakisen by proxy. But he'd known it was the hero himself.

Slopping a brushful of paste onto the third strip of paper Lydia decided that the one person who had a right to know the truth was Procne, who had wept there, beside a stranger's grave. Anyway, she'd love it—that was drama, in the Newbury style.

In fact there'd been two heroes, Aaku and Mrs Newbury, but she'd been made real and solid till her last evening, whereas he'd been made into a sort of ghost long before he died, only his name any use, and his ability to make good *varosh*. His duty had been to become a legend. All that had mattered was the lies that could be told about him, first the imaginary escapades and then the imaginary sufferings. Bloody old men! The worst of it was that they'd become so immersed in their own falsehoods that they'd needed to carry them to the sentimental end of that awful funeral. Really it would have been more honourable to tuck Aakisen away in the rose-bed. But that would have denied them the last chance to summon a lump into their scrawny old throats. Bastards!

However . . . this strip of paper seemed almost to float itself into place, confirming like an omen the rightness of Lydia's choice. All governments, to her, were abominable, but not equally so. She didn't care whether there was any logic in her instinct to support the tiny and defunct government upstairs against the vast and far-reaching neo-Stalinist engine in the Kremlin. She simply knew that their smallness made them incapable of more than little lies and minor mischiefs, whereas in Russia there were probably ten thousand Aakus and a million Mrs Newburys. Perhaps she would mull the problem through with Richard one night; he liked large and abstract questions (think first, fight afterwards, the soldier's art) though Richard himself preferred trains of thought that didn't rattle towards the trenches of action. But Lydia's main mode of thought *was* action. Her dealings with Superintendent Austen confirmed her belief that the government of Britain was only marginally better than that of Russia, because an historical accident had left the individual citizen with a little more power against it; but the police state was there, waiting to be released into domination, like a djinn in a bottle.

So, slowly, her anger with the old Livs and Paul settled into an almost pleasurable displeasure with them. They had behaved disgustingly, but that was the nature of governments, and at least their crimes had been crimes against the dead. To embarrass them would be to help the Kremlin. Her choice to say nothing had stood the test of action.

The papering continued to go well; but no old house has a true right-angle anywhere in it; in every corner each wall meets its neighbour on a slight skew, so that if you simply run the strips on round it you find that what was a vertical on the first wall has become a slant on the second. Lydia was sliding in a neat gusset to turn the corner towards the door when big feet banged on the stairs and a uniformed policeman bounced into the room, a large young man, excited as a puppy.

"Oh," he said. "Sorry. Seen the super?"

"Upstairs," said Lydia. "Were you the chap who was looking for Mr Roberts, the gardener."

"Not me, ma'am, but I hear there's no sign of him."

"Damn," said Lydia. She hadn't particularly wanted him to do anything, but his absence was disturbing, a symptom of disorder setting in in an area where she thought she had created order.

"Seeing you," said the policeman and charged off like a schoolboy looking for Mum to tell her that he's down to play for the under-twelves on Saturday. His overt excitement reminded Lydia of something that she had barely noticed, but had somehow registered, during her interview with Austen. He had been excited too, and so had Eissmann. But Aaku had died of cancer, and Mrs Newbury of a fall—there was only this complicated and unnecessary mess to be cleared up, and where was the excitement in that?

Next time feet rattled on the stairs she was on the ladder, measuring for the strip that would have to run down beside the door and half-way across the top of it.

"Hang on," she called. "I'm on the ladder just inside. I'll

126

be about a minute. Why don't you put the kettle on for some coffee?"

There was no answer. When she took the ladder away Austen and Eissmann heaved into the room with solemn tread. Even though her head was full of figures Lydia could sense that their mood had changed.

"Now, madam . . ." began the Superintendent.

"Wait a sec. Just let me write my measurements down." He sighed, but said nothing.

"OK," she said, picking up her scissors.

"Now madam, I am saying this because I don't want any misunderstandings and difficulties later. With a more co-operative citizen there'd be no need for me to become this formal at this stage, but I want you to understand that a serious crime had been committed and it is part of my duty to question you. You are not obliged to say anything unless you wish to do so, but what you say may be put into writing and given in evidence."

"Seriously?"

"This is a serious matter."

"Christ!"

"Now . . ."

"Wait a minute."

Lydia took the scissors off her fingers slowly, as if she were peeling off a glove. Her first thought was to wish that she owned a tape-recorder. As a next best she chose a piece of wallpaper from her heap of scrap, put it on the mantel-piece and wrote at the top "Memo of interrogation of L.T. by Superintendent Austen, Monday April 3rd, Sergeant Eissmann also present."

"OK," she said.

Austen walked over to see what she had written.

"That's quite unnecessary," he said.

"I hope so."

"Well, if you wish . . . My first question is whether you have any knowledge of a sum of money left in her room by Mrs Newbury."

Lydia dropped her pencil. As she scrabbled for it, she wondered how a policeman puts into his notebook, as evidence, an obvious and appalling start of surprise.

"I'm afraid I can't answer that," she said, still on her knees. Austen waited for her to rise.

"When you say you can't answer, do you mean simply that you don't know?" he said.

"I can't answer that either."

He waited again. Sergeant Eissmann was quicker at taking down notes than Lydia.

"Well," said Austen at last, "do you have any knowledge of a will left by the late Mrs Newbury?"

"Same answer," she said, not looking up from her scribbling.

"Let me make this quite clear, Lady Timms. You are not saying that you know nothing about the will or the money? You are saying that you are not prepared to answer questions about them."

"No I'm not. I'm saying I can't."

"But you admit that the will and the money exist, or existed."

"I can't answer that, either."

This time his pause lasted longer than it took Lydia to write down her note.

"You realise, Lady Timms," he said at last, "that in view of your refusal to answer two simple questions I have every justification for asking you to accompany me to the police station for further questioning?"

"And I have every justification in refusing to come. You have to arrest me, formally, before you can make me come, and after that I have an absolute right to refuse to answer questions and to demand to see a solicitor. That's right, isn't it?"

"That is part of the Judges' Rules, yes."

"Judges' Rules, hell. That's part of the law, isn't it?"

"If you say so."

"Well, do you really want to go through all that? I'm afraid it wouldn't get you any further, because those are questions I literally can't answer, no matter how much you banged away at them. If you want to arrest me, I'll come, of course. I imagine you'd give me time to make arrangements for my son to be looked after."

She had no idea whether the threat was real, or whether the mention of Dickie changed his mind (not necessarily out of human kindness, for there were still a couple of photographers hanging about and Dickie was an extremely photogenic kid). She could sense his hesitation as she scribbled.

"You misunderstand me," he said. "I was only trying to point out to you how suspicious your refusal to answer these questions might seem. A serious crime has been committed, and . . ."

"Has it?" said Lydia. "You don't know whether any money or will existed. Perhaps it's only gossip. If they did exist, perhaps they haven't been nicked. Otherwise there's only this stupid business of somebody putting bodies in the wrong place. That's not really a *serious* crime, is it?"

"Some might think so, Lady Timms. But you will have to take my word for it that a crime which even you would recognise as serious has been committed."

"Oh . . . OK . . . well . . ."

"And you still refuse to answer the two questions I asked you?"

"I *can't*, I tell you! Damn! I've forgotten to write any of this down."

"Take a copy from mine, ma'am," suggested Sergeant Eissmann.

"What crime, anyway?" said Lydia.

"I am not obliged to tell you that," said Austen.

"All right," said Lydia. "Look, I've accepted your word that it matters. Will you accept mine that I've got a perfectly good reason for not being able to answer those two questions? I'm sure there's lots of others I could answer.

The moment she'd said it it sounded stupid.

"I think we'll leave it at that for the moment, Lady Timms. I have other enquiries I can make elsewhere. I think it's a great pity that your husband is not here, and I advise you very strongly to talk this matter over when he returns."

"OK."

"Shall I initial your notes of our conversation?"

"Oh . . . thanks."

It was astonishing, when they'd gone, that the L-shaped strip of paper that Lydia cut from the measurements she'd scribbled down ten minutes before fitted. One might have expected the world to be a slightly different shape, after all that.

22

IT WAS IRRITATING not to have finished the papering, but a
relief to be out of the house. Lydia was experiencing all
over again the oppression and despair that had settled on
her when she had first discovered the dry rot, a feeling of
half-mysterious forces working against her, which were
also somehow her fault, so that if she noticed the symptoms
sooner, or traced the trouble to its cause the moment
she had noticed them, then coping with it would have been
cheap and simple, instead of a long, grimy and costly struggle. As she walked along the Crescent the mood began to
lift; a gang of small girls were playing hopscotch; male
pigeons were pouting at coyly circling females; the green
of the new leaves in the privet hedges was a strong as fresh
paint, not yet dusty with urban summer. She began to look
forward to her lunch, a proper lunch, since Dickie was at
home, grilled bacon and peas and . . .

"Hi, Lydia," said a deep voice. For a moment it seemed
to come from nowhere, then she saw that the large white
car by the kerb wasn't parked there, but had Mr Ambrose
in the driving seat. His big head, made bigger by a gold
turban, leaned out of the window. He was wearing dark
glasses.

"Spare me a minute, sweetie?" he said.

"I'm afraid I can't. I've got to fetch my son."

"Ah, come on," he said, patting the seat beside him. "Let
the little bastard wait. He's got to learn some time."

"Sorry," said Lydia. "Is Mr Roberts OK? He didn't come
this morning."

"You've got trouble. Bob doesn't like trouble."

"It isn't anything serious."

The arched eyebrows rose clear of the dark lenses.

"You've got plenty of trouble, Lydia," he said. "I want
to talk to you about that."

"I'm afraid I haven't got time, and in any case it's none of your business."

"Everything that happens round here is my business, sweetie. I hear you've been seeing my little friend Procne."

"That's none of your business either."

"You'd better stop seeing Procne, Lydia. It's not the sort of friendship that will do either of you any good."

There was something wholly infuriating about his manner, his largeness, his calm slouch at the driving-wheel, his apparent assumption of omniscience, his possessive attitude to Procne—even, in the sparkling April noon, his darkness which seemed to challenge her to say something unforgivably racialist about him, which he would then forgive. But before Lydia could decide whether to walk on on without answering or to tell him once again to mind his own business, his manner changed. He had been shaking his huge head slowly to and fro, as if to emphasise the unwisdom of Lydia's relationship with Procne, but suddenly he froze, frowned at his wing mirror, started his car and drove away without another word.

Lydia simply stood staring, then swung round to see what he had noticed in the mirror. There seemed to be nothing, except a nondescript young man in a tan jacket admiring Mrs Tevell's daffodils. She walked on, disturbed more by her dislike of Mr Ambrose than by anything he had said. It was, after all, perfectly natural, if Mr Ambrose's job was criminal rehabilitation, that he should know Procne—a coincidence, but not an impossible one. It was also natural that he should resent the intrusion of an amateur. Lydia even approved, in theory, of his eccentric approach to his job; anything was better than to be just one of the precedent-following, rule-worshipping workers in the official hive, the *them* of *us and them*. But that didn't make it easy to like him. He was a bully, and somehow bullies for the right are more objectionable than bullies for the wrong.

It was just the bad luck of the young man in the tan jacket that Dickie dropped his cardboard Spitfire in the gutter in such a way that as he darted back for it Lydia spun around to check that he wasn't rushing into the road. The young man, unprepared, hesitated much too obviously before turning into the nearest shop which (again unluckily) was an undertaker's. No doubt you could have thought of explanations for it all, including his sudden decision to make an enquiry

131

about a funeral in a jacket like that, but Lydia didn't bother. He was following her.

It was as though a hunter, after a long, blank day in which juicy game had appeared frequently over his sights only to move into cover before he could squeeze the trigger, came towards evening on a sitting target, a half-grown rabbit, perhaps, which he'd normally have let scuttle away but now in his frustration he blasted to bits with both barrels. Lydia's anger, too, had found a target. She astonished Dickie by dragging him into a stationer's and buying him a usually forbidden *Wizard*. It enraged her still more that the man was so incompetent at his job. Now he was actually standing on the pavement outside, wondering where she'd got to. If the police are going to intrude on your privacy by following you on your most harmless errands, they might at least do it with competence. Lydia ran her mind over the opening shots of her onslaught, then walked briskly out and touched his elbow.

"Are you looking for me?" she said.

He turned. His hand rose as if to remove the hat he wasn't wearing. His eyes widened and his mouth opened as if to stammer the beginning of a denial. Then he spoilt the whole campaign by smiling.

"Ah, L-lady T-t-t-timms," he said. "I w-w-wonder if I c-c-could have a few w-w-words with you."

"I want to know who ordered you to follow me here."

"N-no one did. It was my own i-i-idea. B-but when I saw you t-t-talking to Jones I thought I'd better w-w-wait a bit."

He was a bit under six foot, blond and pink and very slight. He looked as though he ought to have grown a footling pale moustache to demonstrate a minimal masculinity, but he hadn't. His hair was cut quite short. His stammer was natural.

"Aren't you one of Superintendent Austen's men?" she said.

He shook his head.

"Then why the hell are you following me about?"

"I w-wanted to talk to you away from the p-police. It's about Jones."

"I don't know anybody called Jones."

"That c-can't be true, if you think about it. Besides, I saw you t-talking to him. The big Indian in the w-white car."

"His name's Jack Ambrose."

132

"Sorry. Yes, it's that, too. And A-ambrose Jones. Do you know what his job is?"

"Something to do with criminal rehabilitation, I believe. He works for a Council of some sort."

"I d-don't know what they call themselves now. I suppose it is a s-sort of rehabilitation—but it isn't like that at all, Lady Timms. Jones is a f-f-frightener."

"A what!"

"A frightener. His job is to frighten people. M-mostly it's to make them leave their homes, so that his mob can t-take them over, but sometimes he frightens minor p-pimps and such, and takes their girls off them."

Procne, thought Lydia, shrinking into herself. *They done him proper—he's in Morocco, last I heard.* She was scared but not terrified. This was the moment which all her life she'd known might leap out at her, the point when she'd have to fight, as a soldier does. Her mind flashed to the weak places in her defences—Dickie, lying on his belly on the pavement lost in a ludicrous strip about a phantom tank; Richard— how much to tell him? When? After yesterday . . .

"Who are you?" she said suddenly.

"Me? My n-name's Tony Bland."

"Oh . . . you write for *Get Notted*?"

"That's me."

"In that case . . . hell, you'd better come home, if you've got time. I'll give you some lunch. Come on, darling, bacon and crisps. Have you been reading the balloons?"

"Sometimes," drawled Dickie, still drowning in the dream. As he crawled to his feet Lydia saw that he'd been lying across a patch of dried dog-piss. It didn't seem to matter just now.

Tony Bland's stammer turned out to be mostly shyness, but partly (Lydia began to suspect) a protective device, a demonstration of harmlessness and ineffectualness, which might even be quite useful for a young man whose purpose was to sieze capitalism by the ankles, stand it on its head and shake the money out of its pockets.

"What do you think of *G-get Notted?*" he asked as Lydia was turning the bacon on the grill.

"I nearly always buy it, but I don't always agree with it. I like what it stands for in principle, but quite often I get angry about the way it sets about things. Last year I was involved in an effort to get a decent nursery school in this area.

133

Your lot quite rightly wanted it further north—in fact I re-signed from our committee about that very thing . . ."

"I know. That's why I c-came to you. You see . . ."

"Let me finish. You did several stories on it, and they nearly always got something badly wrong."

"We've g-got a very small staff," he said.

"Yes, but that wasn't the trouble. The real problem was that you couldn't distinguish between truth and propaganda."

He cut a dainty square of bacon, piled a little mashed potato onto it and decorated it with three peas, so that it looked like a cocktail canape. He put the load prissily into his small mouth, and didn't answer until he had chewed and swallowed it.

"In most cases there isn't any d-difference," he said.

"I know that argument, and I dislike it. But even if you allow it this wasn't one of those cases. I think it might just have been possible to get a school going, in the right place, with enough money behind it, if that's what we'd all been working for. But you didn't seem to mind whether there was a school or not, provided you could throw enough muck in the Council's face. The Council stinks, and perhaps we wouldn't have got the school anyway, but it wasn't up to you to decide that."

She waited for him to answer, but he simply went through his bacon-cutting ritual and nodded as though he'd heard all this before and had learnt to be patietnt about it.

"So you see," she said, "I'm going to be cagey about what you say about Mr. Ambrose. That's all."

Dickie, eating his lunch in his cardboard hide-out, made a curious wheezing explosion. Tony jumped, but Lydia knew the sound well.

"It's all right," she said. "He's just seen a joke with his mouth full of crisps. Don't worry—he'll sweep up. He's very fussy about his own territory, like a badger. Look, if what you say is true, why did Mr. Ambrose take such trouble to provide me with a gardener?"

"How did it happen?"

She explained the absurd half-fantasy about the spy.

"That t-ties in," he said. "There was an old woman died here, wasn't there—Procne Newbury's mother? And now there's this business about bodies being switched. And I hear s-something about missing money—that's not got into the nationals yet."

"Yes, but . . ."

134

"Procne w-worked for Jones's mob. The old woman died from natural causes?"

"She fell off a table when she was drunk. It all came out at the inquest."

"Yes . . . I wonder if you could f-fake that. Never mind. The mob had a reason for being interested in this house, you see. That b-body-switching business doesn't sound their style —too fancy. But perhaps they heard about it, perhaps they knew about the money, perhaps they s-simply wanted to check up, on principle. But whatever it was, they'd enough reason to send a bloke to do a preliminary scout round. You b-bumped into this bloke, and talked to him about gardening. That g-gave them an opening for their usual operation—Jones came round to check, and you offered him just what he w-wanted—a job for one of his men in half a dozen houses."

"It wasn't the same bloke! I *knew* it wasn't! They found an ex-con who knew about gardening and sent him along! But . . . you mean he was supposed to find out which houses were worth burgling?

"They might try that, as a side-line, but their main interest is housing. They w-work it like this. They find a street which suits them and they put somebody into it for a couple of months . . ."

"What do you mean, into it?"

"It varies. One c-case I heard about, they twisted the milkman's arm—showed him a fiddle, trapped him into working it and then threatened to show him up. They p-paid him a bit of cash, too. Sometimes they take a room. It doesn't really matter, provided they can get a toe-hold. You see, their theory is that there's always a few weak points in any community, and if you can find them out you can exploit them. That's w-where the frightener comes in. The sickening thing is how mean they are. They're rich, but they'd rather scare an old couple out of their home than b-buy them out. Usually it's a bit of both. And once they've g-got their men into a couple of houses they can d-do what they like. Up in G-golborne ward they emptied one street in ten months, f-flat."

"It wouldn't be like that here. Quite a lot of these houses are owned by—it sounds awful to say this—people who'd know how to fight that sort of thing. You know, people with money and education, people the police would listen to."

"I d-don't know. They've got big ideas. But they might play it differently here. They might g-go almost legal. You're right on the edge of the p-posh area in Devon Crescent. If they c-could find a few places which owners were thinking of selling, and then just b-bring down the tone of the Crescent a bit, so that it became p-part of the p-poor area, they c-could start to buy up below the market price, and then there might be a bit of a panic, and perhaps they'd pick up some more houses. Then they c-could take their heavies out, and smarten it all up, and sell off, or l-let off, at a big profit. One of the things I'd like to p-prove is that they've got a working agreement with Dice and Dottridge . . ."

"The estate agents?"

"Right. I'm p-pretty certain they have, but if I could prove it that would really shake things up."

He paused, looking almost wistful at the thought of dragging into the open this juicy big slug of a scandal. Dickie came crawling out of his hide-out, still somehow managing to gaze at his comic with one hand and shuffle his plate along the floor with the other. He rose to his feet and moved like a sleep-walker to the sink.

"Honestly, darling," said Lydia. "I think you've been looking at that long enough for now."

"No, I haven't."

"Please, darling. If you stop now and read it again after tea, you'll enjoy it much more then."

"Can I have an apple."

"Of course."

"All right. I'll go and practise my code."

He let go of the comic so slowly that there might have been half-set glue on it, still running in sticky strands out to his fingers after he'd let go. But he didn't seem to sulk at all. Lydia felt a rush of enormous affection as she watched his round rump wriggle into his hide-out. When she turned back to Tony she found he'd picked up the comic and was reading it with serious absorption.

"Hey!" she said.

"G-great stuff," he said, looking up. "My parents wouldn't let me b-buy them."

"Quite right," said Lydia. "I don't usually. "They're mental pollution."

"They're an alternative universe."

"Seriously?"

"Seriously."

"All right, I'll think about it. But stop reading it now, damn you. I want to know what to do about Mr Ambrose. Do you mind that noise?"

136

. — . . — . — beeped the buzzer as Dickie began to work at random round the letters. Sometimes he kept it up for an hour at a time. Lydia found it restful, like the song of a metal bird.

"N-no," said Tony. "That's fine. D-did your g-gardener ask you questions all the time?"

"No. As a matter of fact he was a remarkably silent bloke."

"Oh. That's not so good."

"On the other hand, Mrs Tevell told me that he was a tremendous gossip. She never stops talking herself, so I thought she just meant that he was a good listener. But perhaps . . ."

"That's b-better. I know the t-type. Just what he'd want. Look interested, egg her on a bit with the odd question, and she'd t-tell him everything she knew."

"So he didn't need to ask me anything?"

Tony frowned.

"I d-don't think that's it. I think it's more likely he'd b-been told to keep his mouth shut here. What did Jones w-want?"

"I don't know. He said he wanted to talk to me. He said I was in trouble. But he raced off when he saw you."

"I w-wish he h-hadn't seen me. The ch-chap who was on the job before me g-got a very nasty beating up. And the p-police don't want to know, because we've made quite a bit of t-trouble for them since we started."

"Yes, I read about that. You were right all along the line there, I thought."

"G-good."

"What do you think I'd better do now?"

"I d-don't know what you'd *better* do. I know what I'd l-like you to do."

"What?"

"I think he'll c-come back. N-not while the police are here, l-later. I'd like to get a t-tape-recording of what he says."

"Why should he come here? I have to go out sometimes. And I haven't got a tape-recorder."

"He'll c-come here, because he likes to g-get at people in their own homes. It m-makes them feel they aren't safe any-where. If he t-tackles them outside, they feel they've still got somewhere to run to. We'll lend you a recorder. Do you know how they work? I've got a friend who can fix it all up for you. You've got to be able to set it going without him seeing."

"Hell," said Lydia. "Let me think."

Dickie's nonsense message to nowhere filled the room still. Tony cut up and ate the chilly remains of his lunch, apparently without noticing how unpalatable it had become. His neatness and sensual apathy depressed Lydia. These people, she thought, my natural allies—do I want them in power if that's how they are? Suppose Mr Ambrose were an official in some left-wing group, a frightener for urban guerrillas, would Tony turn one wispy hair? No. But he's not, and he's got to be fought, at some point, by someone. She realised that it was unlikely that anyone would ever be better placed to fight him than she was, herself, now. His earlier victims had been unprepared, without influence, without allies. She was none of these things.

"How did you hear this rumour about money?" she said. "I don't think it's true, but how did you hear it?"

Tony shook his head, knowing but not revealing, just like Austen.

"You've got a friend in the police, haven't you?" she said. He shrugged.

"Oh, for God's sake!" she said. "I'm not going to get him into trouble. The point is that the Superintendent in charge of this body-swapping business has got it into his head that something serious is going on. I think he's nuts, but if he's right then I think Mr Ambrose must be the bloke he's looking for, so really I ought to tell him about him . . ."

"I'd much rather you d-didn't. He'll ju-just fade away and I'll have to start again."

He sounded quite plaintive about it. No question of his seeing any problems but his own.

"Well, I've got to reserve the right to tell him if I need to. In fact it goes against the grain to tell him one bloody thing. But what I can't afford is for him to find out that I knew who Mr Ambrose really is, without my having told him, and I was afraid your friend in the police . . ."

"N-no, that's OK. What does he mean, *serious*?"

"I wish I knew."

Tony masticated a last, slow mouthful.

"Well?" he said.

"OK," said Lydia slowly. "I don't think there's much chance of it coming off, but I suppose I've got to give it a try."

23

THEY SPENT THE AFTERNOON in Holland Park, Dickie ceaselessly gunning down his mates under the salad-coloured leaves of the adventure playground while Lydia sat on a bench and tried to read her new *Autocar*. There was one dark-haired little Roscius who died a thousand deaths, all spectacular, crumpling into a bullet-riddled heap at one moment and at the next picked off by a sniper as he teetered along a wooden walk-way six feet from the ground. Two pig-tailed girls banged and died with the best of them, but it was noticeable that only the kinder-hearted boys bothered to gun them down. So even at that age men were almost as prejudiced as Father about the feminine role. Lydia made a deliberate effort and dragged her mind away from Mrs Newbury, and Aaku, and Austen, and Mr Ambrose. She took out a pencil and on a blank bit of an advertisement for sparking-plugs wrote "Resolutions: If it's a girl." But the list wouldn't materialise. The dark, cloudy bulk of Mr Ambrose edged continually between her and her imaginary daughter; the ghost of Mrs Newbury gibbered in ancient admonitions, and Superintendent Austen coughed a warning dry cough. That was real. He was walking along the path by the bamboos and when he saw that she had noticed him he raised his hat and walked on. Lydia scribbled out the words she had written. The daughter would have to wait.

When they got home the telephone was ringing.

"Liz?" said Lalage's voice, urgent.

"Yes, darling."

"How are you?"

"Fine. I spent the morning paper-hanging and arguing with the fuzz, and this afternoon I've been watching Dickie shoot his friends. What's up?"

"Oh . . . I just wanted to check . . . I mean, I didn't want to spring this on you if you were feeling . . ."

"Do get on with it. I'm OK."

"Well . . . do you remember I told you Dad had some gen for you about the corpse?"

"That's right. I want to know about that."

"Wait. He's just rung up in an absolute fury."

"Why on earth?"

"Well, he can't see it's not your fault."

"What isn't, for God's sake? Lal!"

"Sorry. I'd forgotten he could get like that. I mean, it's been years. Last time was when Richard left the army . . ."

"I *know* that. Do pull yourself together, darling. Or else tell him to ring me."

"He can't. He's operating on someone's bum. I hope his hand's not quivering still. He wouldn't anyway."

"I can't stand this. I'm going to ring off."

"No. Wait. You asked him to find out whether there was anything odd about the autopsy on Mrs Newbury. Right? He did that. He was waiting to tell you yesterday. Answer, rather huffily, of course not, all above board. Brain haemorrhage caused by fall when drunk. But now they've come round and hauled him out of the theatre and asked why he wanted to know. Tremendous kerfuffle. High horses everywhere. The point is that it *wasn't* all above board. Got it? They'd missed something."

Lydia felt her body gasp, almost as though that were what politeness demanded, while her mind accepted the news. Procne had foretold it, had been right where the world was wrong. It would have been, Lydia now vaguely felt, disloyal to her to be surprised.

"What?" she said.

"They did find something."

"I meant what did they find?"

"Dad said something about a kaffir trick. He was almost incoherent."

"Why didn't he ring *me*?"

"Can't you see, darling? He wants to keep his hands clean. You've made him . . . oh, I expect they'll hush it up, anyway. But he's lost face, and he probably lied to them, and now . . ."

"Does he think that I . . ."

"I don't know *what* he thinks. When he's calmed down a bit . . . Is it serious, Liz? Really?"

"It might be."

"But who on earth?"

"The trouble with this house is that anyone can go in and out."

"Mrs Newbury sounds like a born blackmailer, too."

"Yes."

"At least you're in the clear. And Richard. They can't ... Liz! They can't, can they?"

"Father seems to think they might, doesn't he? You might remind him that I only wanted to know about the autopsy so as to be able to guess how long Mrs N had been on the bottle."

"Oh. Yes. He got that, before this other thing. No time at all is the answer. The bloke who did the job decided that that was why all the alcohol had been absorbed into her blood-stream, and why she got so drunk and fell off the table."

"Only now it looks as if she didn't."

"Oh, God! What did he mean by a kaffir trick, Liz? It rings a faint bell."

"Don't you remember—it was one of his favourite toughen-em-up no-nightmare stories, about witch doctors creeping into huts in the dark and sliding a fine spike into the spinal column? No blood, no wound."

"Oh, Liz, you're so practical. Trust you to remember something like that. I bet you could do it, too."

"Lal!"

"Oh, God! Sorry. Of course I don't . . ."

"You'd better stop talking, darling. Think about money. That'll have a calming effect. Thank you for warning me. Bye."

She put the receiver down to find Dickie standing close beside her, frowning.

"Grandfather told me that, about the spike, too," he said. "What I want to know is where."

"Africa, he used to say. But I don't think it happens any more."

"I meant where on me?"

"Oh. Didn't he show you?"

She remembered the surgeon's fingers, precise as a machine, feeling along the vertebrae. She remembered her own clenched jaw, her violent stillness, determined not to shiver or wriggle, being even then sure that that was what he'd really wanted.

"There wasn't time," said Dickie. "It was Rorke's Drift. Show me."

He stripped his jersey and T-shirt up in a single movement and waited. Lydia counted along the spine, numbering off the hidden beads down the necklace of bone, wondering whether a run-of-the-mill autopsy—with the cause of death so obvious—could be expected to spot this tiny extra wound, and the severed nerves that would carry no more the traffic.

"There," she said, pressing gently. He shivered and wriggled quickly into his clothes. The touch of his body seemed to have restored her blance, so much so that she longed to pick him up and hold him tight on her lap. But he wandered off to the bread-bin, cut himself an erratic slice and spread it thickly with peanut butter. Lydia made coffee, drank it and then slung together a bacon and potato pie for supper. She thought as she worked. OK, I must accept it. Mrs Newbury had been killed. By whom? The case against Lydia Timms. Lydia Timms had been friendly with the deceased, enough to be trusted. She might therefore have known about the hoard of money. She had taken that money and put it into a Post Office account, under her own name. She had destroyed the will of the deceased. She had known and understood the technique of the so-called kaffir trick. She was in severe financial straits, caused by fresh discoveries of dry rot in her house. Furthermore, with the decease of the deceased, the room of the deceased would cease to be leased under a controlled tenancy—a new tenant, a handsome young businessman, lover of the said Lydia Timms's half-sister, and no doubt of the said Lydia Timms on the side, would pay ten times the amount that the deceased had. Furthermore, the said Lydia Timms had concealed from the police several material facts, and had refused to answer certain material questions, and had added one lie. Furthermore . . .

But Lydia's mind wandered down the by-way of working out whether she could in fact have killed Mrs Newbury, without help, in the way it seemed to have been done. You would have to lay her out—no, first, surely, you would have to trick her into drinking a little vodka, then lay her out, then, while the heart was still working, inject more alcohol into her blood-stream, then fake the fall from the table to cover the bruises of the laying-out, then bash her head hard against the fender, and finally do the kaffir trick. She couldn't have done it alone. She didn't know how to lay a person out, for certain, without the use of drugs which would show up in an autopsy; nor was she strong enough to manhandle that sack of a body. As in life so in death, you couldn't get any leverage on Mrs Newbury.

Rolling out the pastry—a brisk and cheerful operation, most days—Lydia reluctantly dragged her mind round to Mr Ambrose. If Mrs Newbury had been murdered, presumably he was the murderer, for some motive to do with Procne. There was no evidence yet for this, but it was the only thing that made sense. So obviously, Superintendent Austen ought to be told about Mr Ambrose. Equally obviously, Lydia wasn't going to tell him. She numbered off her reasons, knowing as she did so that she was only putting up bulwarks round a decision that had been made at a deeper level than reason. First, she didn't want the link with Procne brought to light; second, if Austen had to find out, it would be far better for him to do so from somebody other than Lydia— if she went running to him with the news, he might well think that she was simply trying to drag a red herring across her own trail; third, and most important, it wasn't the murder that mattered, it wasn't Mr Ambrose who was the enemy. The really vital thing, in the long run, was to try to bring into the open the activities of the people he was working for, right back to Dice and Dottridge, if possible. They were the real creators of misery and injustice; they were the people who had moved the Hoods out of Number Forty-six, and broken up the pigeon loft—and had done the same, often with trickery and violence, to thousands of other harmless people, all in the sacred name of property. They were the enemy. Though Tony's plan had only a slim chance of success, Lydia was determined that it mustn't be she who spoilt it. And if it did come off there would be a by-product. Superintendent Austen could hardly refrain from transferring his suspicions to Mr Ambrose, without Lydia having to tell him anything.

Dickie was spending a quiet morning as a submarine waiting to ambush a passing battleship, so Lydia sat down and wrote a careful account of everything that she had done and decided, and her reasons. Then she put it in an envelope and dated the flap and wrote a note to Mr Muxbury, Richard's family solicitor, asking him to certify the date and keep the envelope unopened. Poor Mr Muxbury, lover of trusts and entailments and contingent heirs, dreader of anything to do with the criminal law! If only he knew . . .

The feet on the stairs were heavy but shambling. When Lydia opened the door she found Mrs Pumice outside, with

143

Trevor on one arm and the other carrying a battered suitcase. It took her an instant to realise that if Mrs Pumice had decided to quit she would have left her luggage in the hall.

"Bloke brought this for you," said Mrs Pumice. "Lord, it's heavy."

"Oh, thank you," said Lydia, taking it. "I expect it's some books I wanted."

"Can I come in?" said Mrs Pumice. "I sort of got to . . ."

Her voice trailed into hesitation. She looked very nervous and miserable.

"Come and have a cup of coffee," said Lydia. "Shall I take Trevor for a bit?"

But Mrs Pumice clung to him and came very timidly into the room, as though expecting, somehow, to be punished for being there at all. She jumped violently when Dickie torpedoed her. Lydia took her arm and settled her into Richard's big arm-chair. Trevor, despite his suety appearance, was sensitive to his mother's mood and looked on the verge of wailing.

"What's the matter, Mrs Pumice? I hope the police haven't been pestering you. You mustn't let them. They haven't any right."

That only seemed to make it worse.

"Oh, oh," sobbed Mrs Pumice. "You been so kind to me and I went and told 'em."

"Told them?"

"Oh, oh, if it had been anyone except Princess Anne! She's so lovely. You oughtn't to have took it. Old Ma Newbury really loved that wedding, she did!"

"Honestly . . ." said Lydia.

"Oh, oh," said Mrs Pumice.

"Boom!" said Dickie.

"Shut up, Dickie," said Lydia.

She settled herself on the arm of the chair and put her arm round the throbbing shoulders. Dickie emerged from under the table, flat on his stomach, and using only his toes propelled himself to his cardboard cave. Trevor watched him with suspicious eyes.

"Listen," said Lydia. "As far as I know Mrs Newbury didn't leave anything to Princess Anne. I can't tell you exactly what she did leave, because it isn't my secret, but I promise you I haven't taken anything, and you haven't done any harm, really you haven't."

But still Mrs Pumice sobbed. Lydia found her impatience

at such feebleness tinged with envy. To be able to cry so easily, for so little. To be able to collapse in tears, and refuse to cope, and let the tide of the world drift you wherever it willed, instead of having to swim all the time against its hidden and unpredictable currents. It was a gift, of a kind.

"Oh, oh," sobbed Mrs Pumice, "then I'm worse than what you are. Oh, oh."

24

THE SUITCASE contained an absurdly large tape-recorder, sensitive no doubt, and capable of recording a good couple of hours of incriminating talk, but impossible to hide in the Timmses' sparsely furnished room. In the end Lydia put it under the floor-boards, with the microphone in an empty tin of scourer standing quite plausibly below the sink. She thoroughly enjoyed constructing a trigger mechanism to set the thing going, with a rat-trap lashed to the recorder-box and set so that its arm, when the trap was sprung, came down across the "Start" and "Record" buttons; she padded the buttons up with foam rubber, so that the arm of the trap could get at them and at the same time not make too loud a click. After some thought she decided that the best way for her to spring the trap was by some definite action, rather than trying to do it unobtrusively. So she led a length of black button-thread up from the bait-points of the trap, between two floor-boards, and fastened it to the flex of the telephone so that a jerk on the instrument was enough to release the arm. She reasoned that it was entirely plausible that she, when threatened, should attempt to use the telephone. If Mr Ambrose let her she could jerk it herself. If he prevented her, the struggle would be enough.

That was about all she did enjoy over the next few days. Superintendent Austen questioned her every day for a week. He took to arriving unannounced, almost sliding into the room as if hoping to catch her in some incriminating posture, actually counting the missing money, or reading the missing will. She didn't see him outside the house again—perhaps the momentary glimpse in Holland Park had been a coincidence—but she did spot the curly-haired young man with the side-burns a couple of times. He was much better at his job than Tony, so she got no chance to accuse him. In any case, she reasoned, it wouldn't be a bad thing to have him about just in case the frightener, Mr Ambrose, attempted something in the open.

The interviews with Superintendent Austen became a sort of ritual, with the same questions and responses. Lydia didn't make the old mistake of elaborating, either on her lie or the truth. Superintendent Austen didn't think of any new questions, but on the third morning there was a variation in the ritual. Once more he had asked her about the money and the will, once more she had told him she couldn't answer, once more he had asked whether she had discussed the matter with her husband, once more she had told him to mind his own business. Then he said "Lady Timms, I have no need, I am sure, to tell you how severely the law treats any attempt to interfere with witnesses."

"What on earth do you mean?"

"I mean what I say. I must advise you in the strongest terms not to attempt to interfere with witnesses."

"Heavens! You don't mean Mrs Pumice?"

It was not in the Superintendent's nature to admit even that.

"I'll make a statement about that, if you like," said Lydia. "Ready, Sergeant? Mrs Pumice came to see me, apparently to apologise for telling you about a will and some money that Mrs Newbury was supposed to have left and I was supposed to have stolen. I told her I hadn't stolen anything. That's all. Now, listen to me—Mrs Pumice is very young and she hasn't had much luck in her life. You've got to leave her alone. She simply isn't up to hours and hours of interrogation. If you try that she'll get scared and run away, and then she's bound to get into trouble."

"She has nothing to be afraid of," said Superintendent Austen.

"People like Mrs Pumice have everything to be afraid of. Oh, you make me mad, the way you can't see it!"

"If you would tell me the truth about these other matters there would be no need for me to question Mrs Pumice."

"Can I have that in writing?"

"What?"

"Your threat to subject Mrs Pumice to endless questioning in the hope of making me change my mind."

"I made no such threat."

"Well, that was what it sounded like."

He hesitated, shrugged and retreated into the old ritual. That was almost enjoyable, but the rest of the periods of interrogation were merely dull, dull with the added tension of Lydia having to stay fully aware throughout them in case some variation of phrase might trap her into a casual admission. Too fidgety to begin a major job, she settled to the finicky and boring business of stripping antique layers of paint off the banisters, and finding that the wood underneath was too battered to be worth button-polishing and would all have to be stopped and repainted. That meant hours in gawky postures on the stairs, apologising every time one of the tenants wanted to get past with an armful of shopping or a pram.

Spring turned chilly, and the draught up the stairs made the job beastlier yet. Usually Lydia disliked having to stop and chat when she was working, but it was pleasant when Mr Obb came slowly up and stood watching.

"I wonder whether that was once Livonian pine," he said. "We had quite a good trade in timber, once."

"I don't imagine you can tell," said Lydia, peering at the straight march of grain over the bobbles and flutings. "Do you know, I read somewhere that at one time in the last century pine—deal, we call it—was so fashionable that it became more expensive than oak."

"We have good oak woods also. Just now they will be all yellow with their little flowers. My father used to say that winter was a prison for the earth, locking it in walls of frost. But in spring it broke free and was happy. You do not know what spring is like, because you have never known a real winter. You do not know how the world smells, so fresh, so young, in spring."

"Do you know—you can't smell it now because of this foul stripper I'm using—but I noticed the other day when I was sanding a bit that you could still smell that it was pinewood, after eighty years. It smelt a bit like your *varosh*, in fact."

"Ah, you have not tasted real *varosh*. The stuff we drink here is *ersatz*."

"I liked it."

"One day, again I shall taste true *varosh* . . . Lady Timms, I must discuss with you some time our lease. It runs out in October, I believe."

"That's right. I hope you're staying. But I'm afraid rents have gone up a lot in the last few years. I think perhaps we'd better get some independent person to arbitrate a fair rent."

"Oh, the rent we can manage, but would it be possible for

us to occupy more rooms? If we could perhaps incorporate Mr Vaklins' room, and . . ."

His sad, pale eyes flashed queryingly to Dr Ng's never-open door.

"I don't know about that," said Lydia. "I've made one attempt to shuffle the tenants round, and they dug their heels in. But if there are any vacancies before October of course I'll think about it."

"You are very good, very good," said Mr Obb. "I must go. Very good, very good."

He smiled with extreme sweetness and went murmuring up the stairs. Lydia felt even more dismal as she returned to her dreary chore.

But worst of all was not being able to be frank with Richard. She was quite sure that she was right not to tell him about Mr Ambrose. He had his Bar Examinations in five weeks and was already intensely nervous about them. How could he hope to do decent work if he was worrying all the time about what might be happening to her at home? And though he might respect her decision not to explain to the police about Mr Ambrose, it was impossible that he would agree with it. So she couldn't tell him, but all the time she felt the lie inside her, corrupting her, growing bigger, slowly rotting, strand by strand, the web of love that held them together.

For instance, when they lay talking in the dark she found herself growing tense and wary as the conversation edged towards the secret. When Richard had found Mrs Newbury's body the shock had been like a mental wound, tearing open the half-healed tissues and letting him see again the raw, repulsive innards of his breakdown, three years ago. Now the wound had closed once more, leaving only a sort of itch which he liked to tease as he relaxed.

"I had lunch with Tommy Norris to-day," he said one night.

"Oh? What's he doing? How did you run into him?"

"He's still at the FO, Department 14."

"Isn't that counter-intelligence?"

"Not exactly. They work with counter-intelligence a lot, because their main job's keeping an eye on what foreign embassies in London actually do with their time. I met him on the tube, but I think he rather arranged for it to happen."

"Oh. What did he want?"

(The first twist of the tension-screw.)

"Just checking up, I think. They seem to want minimum fuss. He didn't tell me anything, much, but . . . you know..."

"All right, he didn't say anything but he allowed you to gather. What?"

"Umm. Put it like this. I think there's a bit of a power struggle going on in the FO. Alec Home wasn't the only one who had a lot of face invested in the Baltic States. I'm pretty certain Tommy knew it was Aakisen in the box—by the way, he let on that Obb pulled a fast one there. Apparently when there's a wake the undertakers have a duty to satisfy themselves that they've got the right body in the box before the funeral, but Obb told them that Mrs Newbury's room was Diplomatic ground, so it didn't apply . . ."

"It will be soon, if I let it. I don't mean let it, I mean let it."

She could sense his smile in the dark. He had always enjoyed her tendency to stray into all the homophonous quags which bestrew the meadows of our language.

"Dr Ng's leaving," she said. "He came and saw me this morning when I was doing the stairs, dressed in his best white suit and taking those yellow gloves on and off the whole time. He was terribly nervous. He must have thought I wasn't going to let him go."

"I'll miss him. Why's he going?"

In fact nobody ever saw Dr Ng. He wasn't a real doctor, but had been sitting various medical examinations without success for the last twelve years, so they gave him a courtesy title. Richard had a strong fellow feeling for him, as another late-come student.

"He's come into money. He wants more room, so that he can bring his family over."

"That makes two."

"What?"

"Two lots of tenants who've come into money. Mrs Pumice."

"She doesn't count. Don sent it."

"Umm. How did Dr Ng get into the conversation?"

"If I let the Government have his room they could move their door to the top of the stairs and include that and Paul's room in their territory."

"What makes you think they'd want to?"

"Something Mr Obb said yesterday. I met him on the

stairs. At least doing banisters means I see a bit of the tenants. It's a bloody job."

"You're marvellous. I'll do some at the week-end, if you can find a place where bad workmanship won't show. What did Obb say?"

"Well . . . he started talking about what Livonia's like at this time of year, very strange and a bit weepy. Then all of a sudden he said that when the new lease was agreed they could do with a bit more room. It's only a year since they were talking about looking for somewhere smaller."

"Umm. So they've come into money too. I don't like it." (Another twist.)

"What do you mean?"

"I don't know. Has it struck you that Mrs N's fingerprints would have been on those bottles anyway, if she brought them home? But if they were empties the Government had used, then Linden's would be on top of hers?"

"I know. What's that got to do with Dr Ng's room?"

"I don't know. It's just the way Tommy was nosing about. You don't think . . . this is quite mad. Suppose they wanted to expand, and wanted to bury Aakisen . . . that's two motives for bumping off Mrs Newbury."

"Oh, rubbish!"

"Your friend Diarghi told you that Linden had all sorts of little ways of making people die from apparently natural causes. And didn't Lal say she thought there was something going on, to do with Paul?"

"Honestly, darling, they're such incompetents. I was thinking only the other day how I'd have tackled it, if it had been me, and I decided I couldn't."

"Paul's pretty handy. I've decided I don't care for him, you know."

"Darling, this is nonsense. I mean, Lal was talking about currency fiddling, though she couldn't see how it would work . . . are they all in it? Do you need extra rooms to fiddle roubles? It's all much too fancy. The world isn't like that. You'll tell me next it's an FCP."

"Umm. Somebody killed her."

"Well, I think Procne must have told her something in one of those telephone calls, and she must have tried to use it for blackmail purposes, and that was that."

"Have you told Austen?"

"I can't. And in any case I won't. I'm not sane about that man."

151

"Perhaps I'd better."

"No!"

"What's up, Liz?"

By will-power she resisted the tightening screw, disciplining her limbs muscle by muscle into slackness.

"Sorry," she said. "Cramp."

"You must eat more salt."

"That's just the sort of pseudo-science you learnt from your nanny."

Richard loved reminiscing about his nursery, and did so now, apparently without a thought that they had only a few moments back been talking about a murder done under their own roof and still not solved. Or perhaps he was using his old technique to put the notion out of his mind. At any rate, Lydia was glad to lie half-listening to him and half-trying, in fits and starts, to make more coherent sense of her growing certainty that Mr Ambrose had come to "frighten" Mrs Newbury and had finished by killing her. She was sure that coherent, practical thought would fit in the missing elements, the empties, the alcohol in the bloodstream, and so on. But her thoughts wouldn't cohere. She kept dipping in and out of dreams, all irrelevant. It wasn't until she was truly asleep that she dreamed anything that she could remember next morning: she was hacking plaster off a wall when, between stroke and stroke, the untouched plaster bulged and fell away, and the brickwork crumbled outwards leaving a smoking orifice out of which Mr Ambrose stalked, on tip-toe like a dancer, all covered with strands of grey mycelium which twitched like tentacles and reach towards her own flesh. The dream woke her, and she heard by his breathing that Richard was also awake.

"Nightmare," she said, reaching for his hand.

"Yes," he said, mysteriously, pulling her close, whether for his comfort or hers she couldn't tell.

25

HE CAME NOT AS A MONSTER from behind the wall, nor as a voice in the telephone saying that Dickie would never come home unless . . . but standing on the front doorstep in a green turban, pressing the bell, looking solemn and respectable like a charity collector for an already prosperous Maharishi. It was mid afternoon. Dickie was home from school. Superintendent Austen hadn't visited the house for a couple of days. Lydia's impulse to slam the door was very strong.

"Oh, hello," she said. "Where's Mr Roberts? We've missed him. I hope he's coming back."

"I have tried to repersuade him," said Mr Ambrose gravely, "but when he learnt that you had refused to talk to me he was most hurt. I've been a very good friend to him, you know."

"I'm sorry—I really didn't have time that day."

"You have time now."

"Well, I suppose so," she answered, though it hadn't been a question. "Shall we go downstairs?"

She had hardly time to stand aside as he pranced over the threshold. He was already at the top of the stairs by the time she had shut the door.

"Mind your head," she sang out. Mr Ambrose was tall enough to give the warning some point, but really it was only part of Dickie's spy-game, a code-word meaning "Take cover". With most visitors Dickie would have scuttled into hiding at the first footfall on the stairs, but Mr Ambrose seemed to float down with no noise at all. At the bottom he turned the wrong way and strode into the chaos of what was now Lydia's workshop and timber-store. She took that as a good omen; it was the kind of unsettling trick that he deliberately worked on other people. Only he didn't seem to mind.

"Sorry," she said, holding open the right door. "We've

switched it all round since you were last here."

"You have sold your bed?" he asked, standing in the doorway and peering around.

"No. We've got a separate bedroom now."

"You are luckier than most of my friends, Lydia."

"Yes, I know. Milk?"

"Hot. A large cup."

"I'll put it on. The big chair's more comfortable than it looks."

"You have it then. I'll sit here."

While Lydia lit the gas and put the saucepan on he picked up an upright chair and flicked it over to the shelf by the telephone. Slowly, hitching up his trousers with great delicacy so as not to spoil the creases, he settled onto it. It was a performance, a demonstration. He was master and could choose his own ground and take his time about it, picking in the end a place that commanded both the door and the telephone, cutting her off from the world. Lydia perched herself on the arm of Richard's chair. Mr Ambrose said nothing, but looked round the room as though he were memorizing its contents for a game of Pelmanism.

"I think you were trying to warn me about something," said Lydia at last.

"No."

"Oh. You said I had trouble. I'm sure you did."

"That is your own affair, Lydia. You told me so, and I believed you. How can I do my work if I do not believe people?"

"What exactly is your work?"

(It was a nuisance to have reached this stage without having had a chance to trip the rat-trap, but the opportunity to ask so bluntly might not come again.)

"Ah," said Mr Ambrose in episcopal tones, "I could tell you that that is *my* own affair, but it is not, because my work is helping other people, advising other people."

"You mean like the Probation Service?"

"Sometimes I work with the Probation Service."

"Who actually employs you? Are you part of the Borough Council?"

"I work for a private charity, the Citizen's Council Trust. We call it the Council. We prefer to work without publicity, so you will not have heard of us. We specialise in housing problems."

"Are you a registered charity?"

154

"Why do you ask, Lydia? I am not begging for a subscription."

Tense though she was, some body-clock clicked. Lydia dashed for the cooker and caught the milk just as it rose. She blew on it to break the uprush, poured it out and carried it across to him. As she did so she felt him watching her, felt the pressure of his personality focussed tightly upon her, building up moral dominance. His many-ringed fingers gripped the hot mug without flinching. The rings had sharp outlines on the fat, dark flesh; a sideways flap of the hand would rip a face open in half a dozen places, but Lydia was sure he didn't often need to do that. The feel of the man was enough; there was this switch or stop marked THREAT, which he could pull and at once the threat boomed out of him, without his needing to do or say anything.

"Hang on a moment," she said. "I have got to make a phone call. My sister will be going out later, and I can't put it off."

"Yes you can, Lydia. Your sister must wait."

"She can't. I told you she's going out."

"Then she will wait longer."

"Really, Mr Ambrose . . ."

"Do not use that voice to me. I have taken the trouble to come here to tell you something of importance. I find it intolerable that you should prefer to chatter to your sister."

Lydia hesitated an instant too long. If she had moved at once for the door she could have got there, but the knowledge that Dickie was still hidden in the room, and the determination to trip the rat-trap made her dither, although she knew that the encounter was now out of her control. She had a half-notion that if she made for the door Mr Ambrose, impeded by his mug, would move into her path and thus give her a chance to grab at the phone. So she walked deliberately in that direction. But he was far faster than she'd bargained for. Before she'd taken a couple of steps he had put his mug on the shelf by the telephone, risen, lunged and caught her by the elbow. A flick of his wrist spun her against him with her shoulder in his chest. His stance seemed as solid as a cast-iron pillar, though he was resting all his weight on one leg while the other locked round hers. One hand gripped both her fore-arms behind her back. The hold was gentle but completely firm, like that of a vet examining a wounded bird. Close to, she discovered he used scent. He smelt of wild honey, not strongly but piercingly. The whiff of it seemed to reach in to her, all along her veins.

"Let me go," she said. She didn't expect him to, of course, but she instinctively felt that he wanted her to struggle, to scream. So the best thing was to enter, so to speak, a formal protest. The wild-honey scent frightened her more than his touch and his strength. It suggested an element of irrational savagery; but the rest was just an act, a demonstration. She could cope with that.

With a slow movement like a caress he slid his free hand across her breasts, down her ribs, till it reached her own hand. Carefully he began to bend her third finger backwards until all the tendons were fully stretched.

"Stop it," she said quietly.

He smiled, gave the finger a well-judged extra tweak which made pain twang up to her elbow, then without waiting for her reaction tossed her into the armchair. She'd put good casters on it, so it slid smoothly back under the impetus of her body until it fetched up against Dickie's hide-out. She fancied she could hear his breathing.

"You don't work for a charity at all," she said, scooting the chair back towards the middle of the room. "You're just some sort of hired bully."

"In my work I sometimes need to restrain hysterics. It is a melancholy business."

"I don't believe you."

"You're a fool, Lydia. You think you can buck the system. You've got a very nice set-up here, nice hubby, nice kid, nice tenants. Why should you want to spoil all that?"

Lydia said nothing. Mr Ambrose moved back to his chair, sat, leaned forward and put his ringed fingers together, like a prissy clergyman explaining some point of doctrine.

"It is my experience," he said, "that citizens who misbehave do not get away with it. They are not directly punished, but the good Lord strikes them down in their pride and obstinacy when they least expect it. I remember a young man who started to tell lies about some of my friends, and shortly afterwards he became involved in a fight in a bar and was very severely hurt. I can remember many such cases. A busybody interferes in the life of an unfortunate young woman, and shortly afterwards her own son is knocked down by a car in the street. I have seen it happen many times."

"If you want to make threats you'd much better make them openly."

"To the trained mind that is a hysterical remark. You are too intelligent to become the victim of a persecution complex, Lydia."

"Balls. Your job is to scare people. You put Mr Roberts in to see whether it was worth trying to scare the owners out of some of these houses. You probably decided it wasn't because we'd be able to fight you and that might bring into the open some of the other schemes which your bosses are involved in. Did you have anything to do with Mrs Newbury's death?"

"That old bag?"

He mismanaged the note of surprise, pausing too long before he answered.

"Mrs Newbury didn't die by accident," said Lydia. "And Mr Roberts was a different man from the bloke I first asked about gardening. I believe that Mrs Newbury's daughter worked for your lot, and she used to phone Mrs Newbury once a week for a long chat. She probably told Mrs Newbury a lot of things which you'd rather didn't get out, and if she did Mrs Newbury might easily have tried to use them. I think that first bloke was doing a clumsy sort of recce. Whether you killed Mrs Newbury or not, you'd need to know what was going on."

Mr Ambrose modulated his surprise into a dismissive laugh, not bothering to make his amusement sound genuine. He shook his head, then leaned forward, suddenly earnest.

"We have good friends in the police force, Lydia," he said. "I hear the old bag left a number of papers which you purloined."

"You hear wrong."

"Lydia, Lydia, some of the things you have said about me suggest that you have been listening to lies, or reading lies. But it is true that poor little Procne used to phone the old bag, and Procne is a great liar. I need to know what she told the old bag, and what the old bag wrote down. There was some money, too, wasn't there? That belongs to my friends. Where is it?"

Despite her vulnerability and her failure to reach the telephone Lydia felt that she still had some control over the situation—rather more, in fact, than when Mr Ambrose had worn his facetious mask of charity. She'd actually gained ground. The memory of the wild-honey scent began to recede. And if Mr Ambrose felt as earnest as this about the imaginary blackmail material, it became increasingly plausible that he, or someone else in his organisation, had earlier eliminated the blackmailer.

"Your friends in the police haven't kept you up to date," she said. "I believe that the witness who told them about Mrs Newbury leaving something has now decided she made a mistake."

"The power of landlords over tenants is very great."

"Nonsense," said Lydia, stung to be equated with the type of landlord Mr Ambrose worked for. "In any case, suppose there had been some money, I would have thought it belonged to Mrs Newbury's daughter."

"Ah, our mutual friend, little Procne," he said. "I wanted to talk to you about her. That is the purpose of my visit. When I spoke to you, and you were too busy to sit with me in my car, I did not then know that you had stolen this money of ours. I was merely concerned to point out what damage you might do—would *certainly* do—both to her and your own family by . . . Ah, Lydia, Lydia, you took this money so that you could give it to little Procne when she is released. A sentimental theft. I see."

He sat for a few seconds moving the tips of his fingers against each other and clicking his tongue quietly.

"I hate butch women," he said. "I think I must teach you a lesson."

He reached for his untouched mug of milk and looked at it.

"Skin," he sneered. He poured the milk out on the carpet. "And a cracked mug. Unhygienic."

He put his thumbs into the mug—Dickie's old mug with a steam threshing machine as the design—and pulled it apart. He dropped the pieces in the mess of milk.

"What on earth do you think you're doing?" said Lydia, rising.

He leaped up, grabbing his own chair so that for an instant Lydia thought he was going to hit her with it. But he simply thrust her back into the armchair and stood over her, legs wide. She opened her mouth to yell.

"You scream for help," he said, "and I break your neck. You need some new furniture, Lydia. This old stuff is no good."

He plucked a leg out of the chair and tossed it away, disgustedly. Then with no visible effort he broke the back of the chair across his knee.

. . . — — — . . . sang the metal bird. . . . — — — . . .

158

"Stop it! Stop it! Stop it!" yelled Lydia, crazily hoping to drown the sound.

Mr Ambrose stepped back, nostrils flaring, then dashed at the pile of boxes, tearing them violently from each other and leaving Dickie naked to the world with his hand poised over the key. Even in her fear for him Lydia shared the shock of his finding himself in a world where the brutal enemy did discover the hero's hide-out. She jumped up, tense to bite and claw. Mr Ambrose snatched Dickie up by the scruff of his T-shirt and said "Catch". The chunky little body caught her square in the chest but she managed to clutch it as she fell and convert her fall into a sprawl back across the armchair. By the time she had struggled into a sitting position Mr Ambrose was back between her and the door, looking at the transmitter. He dropped it and put his foot on it as if it had been a beetle. The key scrunched sideways. Dickie gasped. The wild-honey smell was very strong.

"I was wondering where the little bastard had got to," said Mr Ambrose. "Now that's better. You sit quiet, Lydia, or I'll pull one of his ears off. Now, listen to this. You go to the police after, you make any complaint, and my friends will get to him. I've got one particular young friend who is very interested in teaching little boys a bit of a lesson. You get it? Where'd you find these pans. They're trash."

Lydia was particularly proud of her cooking pans because none had cost more than tenpence. She'd picked them up over the years off junk stalls, and even out of skips. She'd straightened dents, found lids that fitted, rivetted handles firm, scoured all shiny. They were part of her personality, far more cherished than any row of matching copper-bottomed pans at eight quid a go could have been. Mr Ambrose snatched one off the shelf, twisted its handle free, bent one side inwards and crumpled the rest together almost as though it had been foil. Think, Lydia muttered to herself. Think. She felt Dickie stir in her arms as the catatonic tension of fear became the willed tension before action. Mr Ambrose pulled the saucepan shelf off the wall—with something of an effort, Lydia was glad to see, because she'd fixed it.

"Pretend to be a bit frightened," she whispered to Dickie under the cover of the clattering pans. "Don't move till I tell you."

No other useful thought would come. She reminded herself that this was a demonstration only, and the sensible thing was to appear to be impressed by it, otherwise he would

159

merely escalate the violence. He kicked a lid across the room, snapped a couple of plastic plates in two, then paused, looking round the room, faintly baffled. He pulled out the sink drawer and tipped its contents on the floor.

"Trash," he said, sounding now disappointed as well as disgusted.

Suddenly Lydia saw his problem. His technique depended on material possessions. The poorest family, living in the lousiest basement, still own things that they value, the half-paid-up telly, the wedding album, Gran's basket of china fruit. You make a token mess, smash a few worthless objects to prove your ruthlessness, then you pick up this treasure, this particular central icon which will make your victim scream "Not that!" But the Timmses had no icons. There were no material hostages.

"Trash," muttered Mr Ambrose again. He stood in the middle of the room, moving his lower lip up over his upper lip and then sucking it down again. Lydia was just wondering why there had been no mess of this kind in Mrs Newbury's room when he suddenly stirred.

"Come here, you little bastard," he said.

"Don't move, Dickie," said Lydia, holding him tight, but beginning to wriggle herself sideways so that she could spring free.

"Come here, I told you," said Mr Ambrose.

"If you touch him you'll get at least six years," said Lydia.

"Leaving the country next week," said Mr Ambrose. "You won't have woken up. Come here, bastard."

Lydia twisted, spilling Dickie into the recesses of the chair, and half rose, shunting the chair back as she did so. Mr Ambrose moved slowly this time, smiling. This was what he had been manoeuvring for, a situation where she should attack him and he could punish her, slowly. Her whole object was to see that it happened in such a way that Dickie had a chance to escape. She didn't notice the door opening.

"Can I help?" said Paul. "I heard your SOS, Dickie."

Mr Ambrose stood still and glanced over his shoulder.

"Out," he said.

Lydia snatched Dickie out of the chair and dragged him behind it. Paul raised her eyebrows at her.

"Please could you go and telephone . . ." she began.

Mr Ambrose moved, springing at Paul like a cat at a bird. As he did so his right hand came flailing round, the rings on it glistening. Lydia seemed to see a collision of bodies but couldn't interpret it because it happened so fast, and because she was trying to work round, taking with her Dickie and the slithery barricade of the chair, to where her kitchen knives hung on their magnetic rack. The house shook with a deep quiver, like the thud of a bomb. But Paul was on his feet, apparently untouched, backing into the middle of the room. Mr Ambrose was turning in the doorway, shaking his head. Somehow he had managed to miss Paul and had cannoned into the door-post.

"Stay in the corner," said Paul. "I'll deal with this nigger."

Lydia did as she was told, taking the chair with her, poised to ram it into Mr Ambrose's path if she got the chance. Mr Ambrose stood by the door as if planning his tactics. With a swiping gesture he swept the telephone off its shelf, ripping the cord from the wall. The snap of the trap seemed only part of the larger racket. He tossed the machine, uncaring, into a corner then began to move slowly, legs well apart, towards Paul. Paul backed away a bit more, watching him. Lydia sidled with Dickie and the chair towards the inner wall.

"Stay where you are," said Mr Ambrose. "Stay where you are."

His deep, gentle voice had acquired a sing-song note, almost like that of a medium in trance.

He feinted a couple of attacks, then moved in with a rush, but this time his left-handed swipe was also a feint; as Paul ducked from it he seemed to duck into Mr Ambrose's other fist as it came looping round in a low arc; but there was no smack of impact as Paul continued his movement and swivelled it to his left while his right arm, flung out at first seemingly for balance, blurred into a whip-like slash. By this time his whole body was close to the floor, twisting so that its energies all culminated in the karate blow that caught Mr Ambrose behind his right knee as Paul flowed away to his own left. The movement was dance-like, formal, and as Paul turned he struck a pose which, though poised and springy, had an artificial and theatrical quality like that of a performer finishing a turn in a ritual dance. And the two thin streaks of blood where the rings had grazed his cheek gave his white face the look of a dancer's mask.

Mr Ambrose had grunted when his blow had missed and the grunt had become a sort of snort when Paul hit his knee. He almost tumbled, clutched at the sink for support, then turned.

"You're thick, nigger," said Paul.

161

Mr Ambrose lurched towards him, but as soon as he put his weight on his right leg he halted. His head swung away from Paul and glared for an instant at Lydia. Then he was rushing towards her, clumsy now, but still very fast.

"Door, Dickie!" she shouted. "Run!"

She threw all her weight on the chair, whooshing it forwards. Mr Ambrose side-stepped but was no longer nimble enough. The seat of the chair caught him just below knee-level and he tumbled thuddingly forwards, grabbing as he fell. Her own impetus behind the chair carried her into his grasp. The huge hand closed on her fore-arm, locked, twisted. She shouted with pain and tried to drag away, but was forced to her knees beside the chair, with her shoulder-joint also twanging with agony. The chair jolted under an impact. Something gave in her shoulder, but then she was loose. She stood up, sobbing and blind with pain, shaking her head.

By the time the mists cleared the two men were locked together on the ground with Mr Ambrose underneath and gripping Paul round the shoulders with one arm. Lydia checked that Dickie was clear of the room, then ran for the knife-holder.

Her best big knife was a French one, with a dull triangular blade and a black wood handle. As she snatched it down she knew it was no use. She couldn't do it. She could not, even in hot blood, choose her spot on the brown flesh and drive the sharp blade home. She looked over her shoulder, hoping that Paul was winnning, but he wasn't. Mr Ambrose was still on his back. Paul had some sort of lock on his legs and had forced his left arm into a spread-eagled position. Mr Ambrose's turban had fallen off, revealing a bald scalp puckered with scars from some old beating-up. Without it he seemed not mysterious at all, no longer the swami of violence, not even Indian, just thug.

Now the whole fight was concentrated into small, shuddering spasms as Mr Ambrose strove to hug Paul's body down towards his own, which would break Paul's leverage on the arm he held. Paul needed his own left arm to force himself back against the gross muscles, but he was losing the fight. Both of them were gasping for breath. A grunt from Mr Ambrose broke the spell.

Lydia dropped the knife and snatched from the shelf beside the holder her blue flour-bin. She took the lid off, ran forward and tilted the flour over Mr Ambrose's face.

There were five pounds of wholemeal flour in the bin. She poured carefully, making sure the first cataract filled the open mouth, then concentrating on the nose and eyes as the big head threshed from side to side. Mr Ambrose began to choke, sending up white puffs of fine flour like the momentary eruptions of a volcano. When his mouth opened to choke Lydia poured more flour into it.

"Stand clear," snapped Paul.

She backed off. He convulsed and broke free, but instantly darted in again, seized a flapping wrist and with a violent jerk flipped Mr Ambrose clean over onto his face. As he leaped in to straddle the back his hand closed round the blubber-protected neck, felt, shifted, tightened. A thumb sank deep but precisely into a fold below the lobeless ear. Mr Ambrose bucked once, feebly, then lay still. Paul seemed to be counting to himself. At last he relaxed his grip and stood up. The blood from the two gashes in his cheek had streamed down his face and smeared his jersey.

"Have you killed him?" whispered Lydia.

Paul shook his head. He laughed in excited triumph.

"Perhaps you have," he said. "That's something they never taught us."

He sounded even faintly hysterical.

"Are you all right?" said Lydia. "Your cheek's a mess. Here's a clean cloth. I'd better go up to your room and ring the police. He bust my phone."

Paul stood, panting still with triumph. Suddenly he seemed to collect himself. He took the cloth from her and dabbed musingly at his cheek, thinking hard.

"Yes," he said. "I don't think you can keep the police out. That would look very strange. Got any cord? He'll come to in a minute."

Lydia always kept spare sash-cord. They used some to lash Mr Ambrose's arms and legs and then to strain the two sets of lashings together. While they were at it Mr Ambrose gasped and choked, then vomited hugely over the carpet. Paul dragged him clear of the mess.

"He'll do," he said. "Here's my key."

Dickie was waiting by the door of the hall, holding Mrs Pelletier's hand. They had the front door open and seemed ready to make a dash for it. Mrs Pumice was peering down from the hall landing with Trevor in her arms.

"It's all right," said Lydia. "We've managed to get him quiet. Thank you for looking after Dickie."

163

"He's been looking after me, more like," said Mrs Pelletier and burst into tears.

"Come up to Mrs Pumice's," said Lydia. "She'll make us all a cup of tea while I phone for the police. You come with me, Dickie."

She shook the two women off outside Mrs Pumice's rooms and went on up with Dickie to Paul's. She hadn't been in since he'd taken it, but she found it almost unaltered. Paul had imported no furniture of his own apart from a big hi-fi system. The ghost of Mrs Newbury seemed still to breathe from the room despite the new wallpaper. Lydia was astonished to find that she couldn't lift the phone to her mouth with her right hand, and that made her realise for the first time how much her shoulder was still hurting, and that in turn made her furious with the police at Sirdar Road when they were slow at grasping that there was any real urgency in the situation. At last the desk sergeant said "All right, madam, we'll have a couple of men round there as soon as poss."

"At once," snapped Lydia.

"Oh, very good, madam."

When she put the phone down she saw Dickie standing by the hi-fi control panel.

"Don't touch, darling."

"But it's supposed to be going. Always. I think it's this one."

He jabbed at one of the buttons.

"Get me a doctor," said Mr Ambrose's voice, thick and grunting, "I got that stuff in my lungs."

"Bother, that's the wrong one," said Dickie, pressing another. "That's right. They're going round now."

The tapes revolved in silence. Lydia stared at them, half hypnotised, half in a daze with the pain in her shoulder. She sat on the edge of Paul's bed and pulled Dickie against her with her good arm. Something was wrong, she felt. Paul had come down because of Dickie's SOS, in Morse. Her brain didn't begin to clear until she remembered that other set of tapes revolving in the musty dark beneath her own floorboards. In the silence a bell rang. She got up and pressed the stop button.

"Come on, darling," she said. "That's probably the police." It felt very strange to be running down stairs actually to welcome them.

26

THE OFFICES OF *Get Notted* were decorated in an amazing green and purple swirling design and smelt of dust, Nescafé and pot. A very dirty girl in the outer office was talking to a smart young negro but stopped the moment Lydia came in and stared at her as though she were an enemy.

"I think Tony's expecting me," Lydia said.

"Through there," said the girl, pointing.

Tony was in a tiny room which might have been a lavatory when the house had been a house instead of a bit of urban blight. He was typing very fast with two fingers.

"G-got something?" he said. "I'm s-sorry. It was m-much nastier than I expected. What happened."

"He dislocated my shoulder," said Lydia. "It'll be all right. I don't think I've got anything much use to you, but I want to listen to something and I can't at home. I hope you've got a spare machine."

She took the tape cannister out of her sling and put it on the table.

"Can d-do," said Tony. "What happened, though?"

"I'll tell you after I've heard this. It depends what's on it. It didn't really start until after most of the talking was over, but I've made some notes about that. OK?"

While Tony fetched and fixed the machine she sat brooding, going over for the tenth time every inch of the living-room in her night-and-day search for the hidden microphone. No new thought came, only the old anger and disgust making it impossible for her to think coherently. In her mind the microphone had become another fungus, creeping into her privacy, rotting her love and trust. Sometimes, if she closed her eyes and tried to relax, she saw against her eyelids a mycelium web of intricate wiring, fruiting all over with electronic sporophores. With another part of her mind she began to be afraid that the obsession might herald a breakdown of her own hitherto solid personality.

At last Tony pressed the "Play" button. There was a crash, then another as the telephone hit the wall. A short, shuffling pause. "Stay where you are," sang Mr Ambrose's voice, trance-toned. "Stay where you are."

"That's him," said Lydia.

"Ps-psychopath?" asked Tony.

The first flurry of thuds and grunts took less than fifteen seconds. Paul jeered briefly. More thuds. Lydia screamed to Dickie to run and now heard, for the first time, his footsteps going, but drowned suddenly by her own yelp of pain. Then more uninterpretable drummings and suddenly, and strangely ghastly even if you didn't know what it was, the sound of Mr Ambrose choking on flour. Proper voices began again, hers and Paul's, both almost in whispers. Then came Paul's Rupert-of-Hentzau laugh.

"That's something they never taught us."

"Who t-taught who?" said Tony.

"I don't know. Shh. We're coming to where I left the room . . . That's tying him up . . . and that's him being sick . . . now!"

But for a long time there was a silence, broken only by a few scratchings. Paul said, "Lie still, Jones," a couple of times.

"How did he know the n-name was Jones?" said Tony.

"I didn't tell him."

She waited, dreary with disappointment.

"Get me a doctor," said Mr Ambrose's voice, thick and grunting. "I got that stuff in my lungs."

"Nothing the prison doctor can't cope with," said Paul's voice.

"Now listen to me, Jones. You're going to go quietly and you're going to plead guilty."

"Bollocks to you, pansy-face," said Mr Ambrose.

"You are a very stupid man, Jones. Have you not asked yourself how there comes to be a man in this house able to deal with you?"

"I'd have got you if that bitch hadn't . . ."

"Shut up and listen. You belong to a little organisation which controls a few streets, and you think you're a king. Now you've run into a much bigger organisation. Much bigger. When your bosses learn about it, do you know what they'll do? They'll pull out. They'll know they can't fight us. They'll tear your guts out if you try."

"Bollocks."

"Jones, we have only recently become aware of you. Listen, you fool. We've had nine days since we learnt of your existence, and already my friends have photocopies of every file in that back room above the Organic Traveller Restaurant. You see? You understand what that means?"

Even through the scourer tin the grunt was audibly one of surprise.

"We know what happened at the Durley Bridge murder, Jones."

Silence.

"I think you have no previous convictions, Jones."

"That's right."

"Good. So you will plead guilty. You will explain that you are obsessed by this girl, Procne Newbury. You will say you resented Lady Timms's friendship with her, and lost your temper. You will get a short sentence, or possibly even a suspended sentence. OK?"

Grunt.

"In either case neither you nor your organisation will make the slightest move against Lady Timms or her family. You will move out of this street. You won't . . . that's the police. I'm going to untie you. You'll go quietly. You'll say you don't know what came over you. Right?"

"OK. I get the message. Thanks."

Feet on the stairs. Paul's voice saying "It's all right, he's coming round . . ."

"That's all," said Lydia. "You don't want to listen to me cleaning up the mess, do you?"

She snapped the machine off. The space round her seemed very small and drab. It wasn't just Tony's office, it was the space round her own life, and Richard's, and Dickie's. She felt very tired of fighting the oppressors, the corrupters, the enemies of freedom and love.

"G-God!" said Tony. "Who was the other bloke?"

She shook her head.

"Leave him alone," she said. "He's out of your league. I'm afraid there wasn't much there for you. I'm sorry. Do you know that restaurant?"

"Kn-know it! Best nut curry in t-t-ten miles!"

"I thought you weren't interested in food."

He almost strangled himself with sudden shyness as the

167

question of his own likes and dislikes was thus dragged to the surface. Lydia could only gather that she had been right, but that for semi-ideological reasons he felt a duty to be enthusiastic about certain vegetarian restaurants. They played the tape through again to let him recover himself.

"What's Durley Bridge?" she asked.

"Miscarriage of j-justice. Years ago. Wrong man hanged. They were still hanging 'em then."

"Do you want to do anything about it?"

"I d-don't know. It's slightly crank territory. Why?"

"Well, if there'd still been someone in prison, we'd have had to. But I'm very frightened of Mr Ambrose now. I'd like to think that somebody still had some sort of hold on him."

"This other bloke?"

"Leave him to me. I've got to go now, Tony. I've got to collect Dickie. Listen, when you do what you're going to do. whatever it is, you'll remember it's got people in it, won't you? People like me and Mrs Pumice and Procne Newbury. Sorry, I know that sounds rude. It's just I sometimes think that you get carried away and forget."

"N-not much chance of forgetting about you. Or P-P-P-Procne. D-different reasons, of course."

"Glad to hear it. Bye."

That evening Lydia sat in her chair. Richard was reading a dismal-looking volume on company law, an aspect of his studies that normally infuriated her, because she wasn't quite able to envisage an industrial society that could be run without it, though its detailed provisions seemed to her almost exclusively immoral. But to-night all her furies were concentrated on her search for the microphone. She had even drawn a careful grid of the room, to search through square by square, because anger had warped all the mental grids she had made.

Dickie came crawling from his improved hide-out behind the bookcase and in complete silence collected a spoon, a clothes-peg, a wooden skewer and two wooden play bricks. He sat on the floor with them, frowning and moving them about. Lydia went back to her grid. Click. Click-click. Click. Click-click-click. Click.

"Bother," said Dickie as his improvised Morse key fell to bits. "I wanted to practise."

"What's the matter, Liz?" said Richard. "You look as

though you'd just won an Aston Martin off a cornflake packet."

"Try using a big elastic band round the skewer and under the block and over the other end of the skewer," said Lydia. "Then you won't need the clothes peg. Can we have a drink, darling? And stop reading that horrible book and tell me I'm a nitwit."

"I can't do that without hearing the evidence."

"Let's have a drink, anyway."

"OK."

"Well," he said. "What about that evidence?"

Lydia was lying on the wrong side of the bed, because of her shoulder. It seemed very odd to be holding the wrong hand. Otherwise she felt marvellously relaxed, simply from having decided that there was no microphone in here, either.

"Darling, you won't laugh at me?" she said.

"I don't know until I see what you say. Sometimes I can't help it. You make me laugh. It's one of the reasons I love you."

"Pig. Do you think I'm really a lesbian?"

He didn't try very hard. She kicked him as he lay snorting.

"Damn you, I'm serious," she said.

"I know you are. It was just the surprise. You didn't give me a chance. You might have led up to it tactfully. If you'd given me a thousand guesses about what I wasn't allowed to laugh at, I'd still have . . . stop kicking me! I'm sure it's bad for your shoulder."

"It is, but it's worth it."

"All right, all right. My face is straight as the equator."

"That's only straight if you look at it sideways. Am I a lesbian?"

"Explain a bit more."

"I've had Austen here again, twice."

"How's he taking things?"

"Not very kindly. I mean, if you're baffled already, it must be a kind of insult to be confronted with fresh bafflements."

"So he accuses you of being a lesbian?"

"Not yet. But he's got on to the connection between Mr Ambrose and Procne, and he knows I've been to see Procne, and I've been wondering what sort of story Mr Ambrose is going to tell. I mean, all the evidence I've got is that he pretended that he was some sort of social worker and told me to stop seeing Procne. If he says he did it out of jealousy . . ."

"This is all very much up in the air, for you, Liz. It's the kind of thing I spend my days fretting about."

"No. It's practical. I mean, it's almost like a piece of machinery."

"Umm. What does Austen think?"

"I don't know. I think he still really wants to prove that Paul and I got together to kill Mrs N, because I wanted the money and he's my lover. That's why I redecorated the room as soon as I could, to cover fingerprints or something."

"Umm. How far could Ambrose take his story? Could he say that you attacked him out of sexual jealousy and that's what caused the mess in the room?"

"It won't wash. I made them fingerprint some of the things he'd smashed, and the telephone and so on."

"You are the original wonder-woman. Anyone else would have been running about screaming or filling themselves up with sedatives."

"I came damn near it."

"That's what's marvellous . . . but why are you bothered about this other thing? I mean it's . . ."

"Being crypto-butch?"

"What do *you* think, Liz. That's what matters."

"What do I *feel,* you mean? I don't think I feel . . . damn . . . you see, I suppose I keep my feelings so battened down that anything like that would come out all changed . . . but it was the first question Procne asked, Richie."

"What you're saying," said Richard in the finicky, thin voice he used for arguing out intimate teasers, "is that Procne—partly because she's a natural animal and partly because she's had a lot of experience—might instantly perceive in you a strand of which you are unaware. Perhaps Ambrose might see the same thing. You feel that this would account for your apparently low sex-drive and your obsession with Procne and your dislike of your father and your passion for doing what most people think of as masculine jobs at least as well as a man can. You are, of course, mainly worried about whether your desire to help Procne and your liking for her are based on this hidden drive. It is the secrecy and uncontrollability of the drive that frighten you. You wouldn't think it at all disreputable of someone else to be a lesbian, or of yourself, if you chose it consciously. But you are alarmed about the possibility of something inside you rebelling against your conscious choices."

"I hadn't thought it out as far as that. I expect you're right. Shall we talk about something else?"

"Not until I've told you I think it's all balls."

"But you don't *know*."

"Look, I do know some things. I've been through some experiences most people have missed out on. I've watched myself falling to bits and then being pieced together again. I know what's at the centre of my world. It's not one great abominable serpent stirring in its dreams that makes the surface heave and erupt. It's hundreds, thousands, of smaller creatures. They're all right, most of them, provided you let them bide where they were created to be. In their natural dark they are beautiful. So . . . Entia non simplificienda praeter naturam."

"Gentlemen don't talk Latin in bed. What does it mean?"

"Look how much it leaves out, the, er Ambrose hypothesis. Here's this girl who's a perfect symbol of all the things you really care about, an archetypal spoilt life. You've got a Pavlov reaction to that sort of thing. And, look, you aren't going to tell me that your fondness for that frightful old harridan Mrs Newbury was crypto-butch? You managed to like her a lot, in spite of everything, and naturally you transferred some of that to Procne . . . has Austen been to see her?"

"I think so. He went before, soon after we found the body, but she won't have told him anything. She'd just clam up, or lie. This time I think he asked her about me. Anyway he asked me about her, quite a bit, and why I wanted to visit her, and so on. He asked me the usual old questions about the will and the money, but he's getting very half-hearted about that, so I don't think she told him what I'd done."

"Pity. I wish she would. That'd take him off your back . . . Liz?"

"M?"

"Come a bit closer, if you can without hurting yourself. If I go threshing about I'll do your shoulder in, but I want to talk to you."

Moving carefully she achieved a position of surprising comfort, curled along his side with her head on his chest. He stroked her hair gently.

"You don't have to go on looking after me," he said.

"What do you mean?"

"I'm OK. I can take my share again."

"Of course you can. You do."

171

"Liar. Listen. I knew you were up to something, those days before Ambrose came. I knew it was important and you were scared. I decided quite consciously I wouldn't interfere —of course if I'd realised quite what you were up to, I *would* have, but . . . can you see that not interfering, going along, trusting, all that was much more of a strain than it would have been to ask? A year ago I couldn't have done it. Do you follow me that far?"

"Yes."

"Well, then, don't you think you ought to tell me what you're up to now? Lie still. Take it easy. That's better. Now . . ."

She told him, slowly, in a whisper. It took a lot of persuasion to make him let her go ahead with it.

27

"SORRY," said Lydia. "The Post Office engineer's just been to mend the phone and I wanted to try it out. Would you like a cup of coffee?"

"Indeed I would," said Paul. "I'll bring Dickie's transmitter down. I've patched it up."

"Oh, you *are* kind. He's out with a friend, but he'll be thrilled when he comes back."

No mucking about this time with fancy trip-cords. Lydia pulled the thread with her own fingers and heard the rat-trap snap. Then she put the kettle on. She was spooning Nescafé into mugs when his head poked round the door. The stitches down his cheek looked like two rows of little black ants.

"There," he said, putting the transmitter on the table. "It wasn't too bad, because I made it tough enough for a kid to knock about in the first place."

The kettle hummed to the boil.

"I thought it stood up remarkably well," said Lydia, pouring out the water and handing him his mug. "The other half was still working, wasn't it?"

He took the mug without a tremor and sat down, smiling.

"I'm sorry," he said. "I hope you'll forgive me. Do you want me to explain?"

"If you can. Where is it?"

He took from his pocket a delightful multiple tool which with a twist and a click became a small screwdriver. He undid two screws and swivelled the toy sideways on its base. The object that nestled in the cavity didn't look like a microphone at all.

"Is it transmitting now?" said Lydia.

"I hope so."

"Surely when Dickie pressed the key . . ."

"Yes, that was a mistake. I devised a beautifully efficient jamming system for my own transmitter."

Point one. If he was telling the truth, he hadn't heard the part of the conversation with Tony about her own bugging system. Curiously this slight gain made Lydia suddenly more tense. He seemed aware of the change.

"You *are* angry," he said. "I'm sorry. You see . . ."

"Switch that thing off first."

His eyebrows flickered up above his pale eyes. He tapped his teeth a couple of times with the screwdriver, then used it to disconnect the microphone.

"That's better," said Lydia. "Well?"

"Does Lalage talk to you about me?"

"Not much. We don't."

"I see . . . well . . . I'm sorry, this is rather embarrassing, because it's going to sound like a declaration of love, but it isn't."

"My heart is already possessed by Another."

He laughed and relaxed, or seemed to.

"I know," he said, "that's part of it. I asked about Lalage because she is often cross with me for talking about you so much. I have allowed myself to become somewhat obsessed with you . . ."

"Oh, that's rubbish."

"No, really, it's true. I mean . . ."

He gestured with absurd and theatrical penitence towards the little transmitter.

"Tell me something, since we're talking about truth," she said. "You remember you told Dickie a story about ambushing a slave-train? Were you really there?"

"Yes. Why?"

"But that happened in Estonia. It was nothing to do with Aakisen at all."

"I changed a few details. If I'd known Dickie then like I do now, I wouldn't have."

"I don't think you're a Liv at all."

"I am, Lydia."

"I think you were one of the guards."

"I'm too young. I was a child, on that train."

He looked broodingly at the little tool in his hands, clicked and twisted it and produced instead of the screwdriver blade a fine steel spike, with which he started to clean his nails, though it was not well adapted for the job.

"I *am* a Liv," he said quietly. "I was a small child when my father died in a political upheaval. My mother took me to Estonia, but she too had been a political activist, so later,

174

at a time of . . . I was taught to call it 'normalisation' . . . she and I were included among dissident elements who were to be removed from Estonia to another part of Russia, for our own good and the good of Estonia. So that was how I came to watch the attack on the train. I saw it between the the slats of a cattle truck. They didn't attack our truck, because they were only interested in rescuing certain elements of their own organisation. Both sides were equally incompetent. Several people in my truck were wounded or killed by bullets from the partisans. On the other hand, the train was booby-trapped with explosives so that we could all be blown up if we were ambushed, but this the guards refused to do. I doubt whether many of those who escaped survived their exposure in the marshes. Some of us, it's true, also died of exposure during the journey, but not nearly so many, and when we reached our destination my mother was given work and I was allowed to live with her. I was also given an education, a very sound one. When my mother died, quite normally, of a brain tumour which would have happened under any political system, I was almost grown up. You see? I could not tell it like that to a child."

Lydia sipped her coffee and thought. Paul seemed to want to talk; she had expected to find him much more guarded and wary.

"About your education," she said. "You said something when I poured the flour into Mr Ambrose's mouth. You said 'That's something they never taught us.' Who were 'they'? What were you?"

He smiled at her and shook his head.

"Well, then," she said. "How did your father die? Did Count Linden kill him? Or have him killed?"

The smile seeped away.

"With a spike like that? Between the vertebrae?"

"You are being stupid, Lydia."

"I need to know. It's all right—I'm quite safe, I think. I've taken precautions. They'd work, I think."

"If you took them, they would. Of course."

"Well?"

"But you are still being stupid."

"What did you say to Mr Ambrose while I was out of the room?"

"Very little."

"You didn't promise him anything or threaten him with anything?"

175

"I told him to leave you alone."

"And then as soon as you get the chance you suggested to me that we should play down what he'd done, in our statements."

"I said I would, provided he agreed to leave you alone."

"And you think he'd stick to his side of it."

"He'd better."

"Paul . . ."

"No, it's my turn. I want to know what's on your mind. You've got some sort of theory, and you want me to confirm it. So you are trying to lead me into saying things which . . . I don't know. Wouldn't it be easier if you told me what you are worrying about and I told you whether you were right or wrong?"

"I'd rather you just answered my questions."

He shook his head, smiling again, but wary now.

"OK," said Lydia, after a pause. "I'll tell you some of the things that are worrying me. Mrs Newbury had a horror of drink, and a horror of empty bottles; and there ought to have been more fingerprints than just hers on the bottles. Then there was that night you made the transmitter and we went to the Russian Embassy—a man called Mr Diarghi told me some stuff about Count Linden and General Busch; afterwards Richard and I decided it was a rather obvious attempt to get me to refuse the renew the lease for the Consulate here, but then Mr Diarghi rang up to tell me he'd got his facts wrong. But he hadn't. I looked them up. Then you've been trained in unarmed combat, and you've got a natural entrée into the Liv set-up here because you own a ship rather mysteriously released by East Germany. Then there was Mrs Pumice's money—she dressed up to go and collect it, and she looked wildly excited, and she was obviously lying about where it came from—Don would never send her more than enough—and it meant that she didn't have to move rooms so you could have Mrs Newbury's room. And only a few days ago she came and told me (but she wasn't at all coherent) that she'd behaved badly about something to do with money in a way which she imagined had let me down. I believe she meant she'd taken that money from you and pretended it came from Don. Then there was Dr Ng coming to tell me that he'd come into money too, and wanted to leave, and he seemed pretty nervous about something. And Mr Obb had been talking to me the day before about renewing the lease, and hinting that he'd like to expand into Dr Ng's room; and he was also in a rather funny state, very nostalgic about Livonia and saying that he'd soon be tasting real *varosh* again, which he could only do if he went back to Livonia. And then there's this stupid business of putting a mike in here. I can't believe your explanation for that, I'm afraid . . ."

"It's true, Lydia."

". . . and then, when you were alone with Mr Ambrose you told him something quite different from what you said just now. Dickie switched your machine on and I heard."

"Not different," said Paul, accepting the half-lie. "Just more elaborate. I wanted to convince him that he'd suffer if he caused trouble."

"And you did that by telling him about the Organic Traveller Restaurant. That had to be true to be any good. How could you have known about it unless the rest of what you said was true?"

Paul hesitated between a frown and a smile, neither very convincing. His sigh was more real.

"I cannot see a pattern in these details," he said. "What is your theory?"

"Look, Paul, I'm not trying to find a victim. I don't believe in punishment. I think you killed Mrs Newbury and I think it was a wicked thing to do, but it's over now. If I could prove it, I'd still only want to use it if you started to mess around with the lives of the other people living in this house. That was your real reason for putting a microphone in here—you knew I discussed with Richard what I was going to do, and you needed to know everything about what the tenants were up to, and my plans for them, because I was in the process of moving everybody round to cope with the dry rot so there were all sorts of possibilities for intervening and gradually taking over the whole house, provided you knew in time. The sickening thing is that it's exactly the same technique that Mr Ambrose's organisation used when they wanted to take over a street. But all that's over now too, and the police seem to be easing up as well. It is over, isn't it, Paul? You haven't been working on Mrs Evans, for instance? I noticed she seems suddenly a bit shy of meeting me."

Paul stretched and almost yawned.

"And you still don't believe I'm fascinated by you," he said. "In the camp where we were taken by that train there was an old man with one leg, a cook. He'd been sent there from the South, almost into India. He used to tell us kids stories about the heroes of his tribe, little chiefs who had fought their big neighbours to hold onto their freedom, little kings with their own little courts who, for the sake of a few valleys, would hold off the armies of two empires which were trying to crush them from either side. And all this was five hundred years or more ago, but their names were still alive on the lips of an old cook sitting by a stove in Siberia. You are like one of those old heroes, Lydia. You have shown me something. I was taught that your view of the world was, at best, a mean type of self-deception, and now I know it is a noble type of self-deception. But even you, Lydia . . . can you explain to me the moral difference between the Russians using physical force to move people to a place which is more convenient for everybody, and you using economic force to move Mrs Pumice to a room which is more convenient for everybody?"

"Mrs Pumice matters to me as a person. I wouldn't have moved her against her will."

"But it was against her will, Lydia. As soon as she was presented with an adequate weapon, in this case a counter-vailing economic force, she refused to go. Those petty kings I was telling you about, they were admirable men, heroes, their names bring a brightness to the eyes of old men and children, but historically speaking all they achieved was to prolong for a couple of generations the miseries of their people."

"Talk about now, damn you!"

He gave a little silent snort of laughter and shook his head. His eyes too had a brightness in them. He was, Lydia suddenly saw, getting a kick out of the situation. She tried to make allowances for what she knew to be her own imperceptiveness about other people, and her tendency to think of them in types—the downtrodden, the oppressor, the insular housewife—perhaps, she realised, it was Mrs Newbury's blatancy of personality, breaking this barrier, that had made her seem so valuable to Lydia. But Paul . . . hitherto she had been thinking of him as the honed tip of a big machine for subduing people, and for killing those who couldn't be subdued. Now she saw there was something else, all sorts of complexities, and that his absurd romantic babble about dead princes wasn't merely a tease, though with part of his mind he was undoubtedly teasing her.

"You don't understand at all, do you?" he said.

"I understand that you're being exploited just as much as the rest of us," she said. "Only you think you aren't."

At last she had surprised him. It was as if a wrestler, poised and balanced, had felt something squirm under his foot.

"Somebody your side wanted a bloody great cock-up," said Lydia. "They decided you were the man to produce it. I wouldn't be at all surprised either if somebody in our own FO had guessed what was going on, and was just allowing you enough rope to hang yourself. There's plenty of that sort of bastard about."

"Now it's my turn not to understand at all."

"Think about it. You were sent here with instructions to infiltrate the Liv Consulate, which you did. This probably started as a minor operation, because it must have been preparing for several years, but when we expelled all those Russian agents it suddenly became more important, because it offered you the opportunity to create a fresh base . . ."

"Lydia, you are being absurd. You cannot seriously believe that if I were a Russian agent I would have jeopardised my task by an unnecessary killing. I say that since you seem to think . . ."

"You didn't even blink when I suggested first time that you'd killed her. And yes . . ."

"But there are plenty of large empty houses in London."

"Not with diplomatic immunity there aren't. When we expelled those Russians we expelled part of a big machine, which needed to work in a single establishment and was geared to having diplomatic immunity. Bosses like the ones you work for can't ever be quite happy about letting agents loose on their own in a capitalist society. Look how you love that car of yours. They must have thought this was a unique opportunity, with an agent already here and ready to start work."

"But don't you see, that would be risking this carefully planted agent?"

"I know. There are two things about that. The first is that I'm sure the original purpose in getting you here at all was to work to discredit the Livs, and if possible all the Baltic Consulates, with the British Government. Mr Diarghi was still working on that, as you learnt that first night you used the microphone—we were still sleeping in here then. When they decided on this new plan they said to themselves that they'd do it in such a way that if it went wrong it could al-

179

ways be blamed on the Livs. That's why you had to kill Mrs Newbury in just that way, so that if the murder was discovered it would turn out to be one of the ways in which Count Linden used to dispose of people. That's quite well known—there were even questions asked about it in Parliament. His motive would have been to provide a funeral for Aakisen. One thing puzzled me for a long time—the Russians must have known for ages that Aakisen was here, so why didn't they say who it was when his body was found? That would have completely discredited the Livs, even if they couldn't make the murder stick. Great national hero, supposed to be fighting and suffering behind the Iron Curtain, actually pottering around in Kensington making booze for a gang of ex-Nazis."

"Well, why?"

"Because this other scheme looked like coming off. I bet it was a near thing, but they let you go ahead in the end. They probably told themselves that even if they set up a spy nest here it would be blown in a few years but there would still be this bonus—the British would be pretty well bound to close the Consulate down then, and perhaps the other Baltic Consulates as well."

Paul shook his head.

"Too tricky," he said.

"Exactly," said Lydia. "But you were the agent. I said there were two reasons for the risk. I very much doubt whether you had permission from your bosses to kill Mrs Newbury. Under the new scheme you were supposed simply to infiltrate the Consulate, buy Obb if possible, and then expand by offering me more rent than my existing tenants were paying, buying them out where necessary. But you like risks. For instance even I could see that you enjoyed the idea of fighting Mr Ambrose . . ."

"It amuses me that you still call him Mr," said Paul. He did sound genuinely amused, too, as he twiddled the deadly little spike between finger and thumb. Perhaps he was enjoying this fight also—same arena, different opponent.

"I'm grateful to you for getting me out of that," said Lydia. "Even though I know you had to fight him. You couldn't have his crowd muscling in on your schemes. But what I was saying is that I think you enjoy risks—you actually need them. You have a romantic view of yourself. Perhaps you told yourself that it would be satisfying to have Count Linden falsely convicted of a murder done by the

180

same means as the murder of your father. Revenge is a horribly romantic idea . . ."

"Horribly?"

"I think so. What you were saying just before about me being like a medieval prince—you meant that as a compliment, but it isn't one. I'm not like that and I don't want to be like that. But I think it is how you see yourself . . ."

"If so, we are the same kind of person. Because you *are* like that, Lydia."

"No we're not! You think you can use people. You don't think about them as people, individuals. There's just you and the rest of the world. Look how you used Mrs Newbury, just as if she'd been a handy piece of timber, one of those planks which are exactly the right shape for the job you have in hand . . . What you don't seem to realise, Paul, is that you're being used in exactly the same way . . ."

"But according to your theory I am acting beyond my instructions."

"That's right. But I bet there's somebody—somebody quite high up in the system—who guessed you would. I know the type. You get them on committees. They're professionals. They don't say much, they just cover their own position and let you go along into disaster. In my case it's usually because they like to see amateurs making a mess of things; but in yours it's because there's a lot of high-ups in your organisation who are bitterly opposed to the whole idea of détente between Russia and the West, and are perfectly happy to engineer a bloody great security row to try to spoil things, provided it doesn't endanger their own position . . . I bet you can guess just who it was, too."

He shook his head, still smiling, but his eyes were angry. Perhaps he really did want her admiration; he didn't mind her thinking of him as cruel and treacherous, but he did mind that she should think he could be used, like a tool, without free will.

"It is funny," he said. "I've always thought of you as a practical person, yet here you are indulging in this enormous fantasy, and it isn't even coherent. I'd expect you to make your fantasies work, at least; but here I am, in your fantasy, threshing around and causing chaos; and yet at the same time things were going very well according to another part of the fantasy. It was only by accident that Richard dug up Mrs Newbury's body."

"That must have been a shock."

"It was. I thought Busch was going to have a heart stoppage."

"But I think she would have got out somehow."

His eyebrows rose in apparently genuine surprise that she should admit to this pocket of blatant fantasy.

"I don't mean physically," she said. "But there are some people you can't ever quite bury, and she was one of those. I wish I thought Aakisen was another."

"This is an absurd situation. It is like a sort of French farce for moral philosophers. We both demand that the world shall breed heroes. You choose that terrible old woman to be yours. I choose you to be mine. Then you accuse me of killing your hero."

"But that's real. You did, didn't you? You brought her down the empty bottles, wiped clean of fingerprints, so that only hers would be on them. Count Linden makes the *varosh*, so taking his fingerprints off might throw suspicion on him. I don't know how you tricked her into drinking some vodka but I know how you laid her out, because I saw you do it to Mr Ambrose. Then you injected more alcohol into her blood stream while she was still alive. Then you killed her the way Linden used, with that spike. And last of all you faked the fall to cover any bruises. Bodies can bruise quite badly after death. I know that. Am I right?"

He looked at her, head cocked on one side, then sighed.

"Let us pursue the fantasy. Let us suppose I did. What then?"

"Don't let's start on that yet."

"No, that's what matters. You said so yourself. Everything else is over and done with, like my father's death. It doesn't matter any more."

"I didn't mean exactly that."

"That's exactly what you said, in effect," said Paul. He had left his head cocked in its teasing attitude, but she could hear in the dryness of his voice that he was only barely controlling some emotion, grief or anger.

"Let us suppose all your fantasy is true," he said. "Let us consider what the consequences are of your discovery. There would have to be some sort of bargain, for your silence. You would not expect an organisation which has invested time and effort and prestige into setting up the system you've imagined—you wouldn't expect them now simply to shrug and go away and not trouble you any more."

"No," said Lydia slowly. "I've thought about that. Organisations aren't machines, though. They consist of people, and people do have free will. I can't see any reason why you shouldn't simply stop working for them . . ."

"Defect?"

"Not if it means working for our side instead, in the same way. We're just as bad. But I'm sure you must have arranged some escape-routes for yourself—escapes from this whole world. If you took one of those, that'd be enough. All I'd need is proof that it was you who'd killed Mrs Newbury, and I'd only use it if somebody else was accused of killing her."

"Then you'd be an accessory after the fact."

"I've got to risk something, haven't I?"

At last he uncocked his head and leaned forward with the bright little spike dangling loose in his hand.

"Doesn't it strike you," he said, "that an organisation such as the one in your fantasy might consist of people who choose to work for it, of their own free will?"

"Yes, I'd thought of that too. In that case I'd still need proof, and I'd still only use it if I or my family or my tenants were threatened by your lot, or again if someone else were accused."

"Have you considered what would happen if my supposed organisation simply withdrew our protection from you, and informed Ambrose?"

"Yes. I'd have to find ways of fighting them off."

"You would lose."

"Still, I'd have to try."

"Suppose, in exchange for your silence and their continued protection this organisation were to accept a renewed lease for the Liv Consulate, including the floor where my room is?"

"No."

"Perhaps they might also be able to arrange protection for Miss Newbury when she comes to live here."

"No!"

"Why the emphasis?"

"You would want to use her. She'd become a tool, a thing, a prisoner again!"

"Lydia, where is the tape-recorder?"

He caught her completely off balance. She felt the blush encrimson her neck and face.

"I have realised almost since we started talking that there must be one," he said. "I think I understand you very well, Lydia. You like to achieve everything by yourself, without help. It is inconceivable that you would arrange for police witnesses."

He sat back, but seemed now not at all relaxed. There was something about the movement of his fingers, playing delicately but restlessly along the line of stitches on his cheek that reinforced Lydia's perception of sharp emotions reacting inside him, like chemicals in a retort—the old anger for the death of his father perhaps, and the stress of facing her and the deeper stress of facing the nature of his own actions, desire for her admiration, fear of his own masters—at any rate, she sensed, the reaction was coming to its climax. Perhaps it was not too late to persuade him to take one of the escape routes. At least she ought to try. The first essential, then, was to show that she trusted him.

"I'm sorry," she said. "You do see? I had to have a hostage. I can't get at the machine but I can switch off the mike."

She rose, crossed the room and kneeled by the sink. It was slightly tiresome having only one good hand to ease the mike out of the scourer can.

"Ingenious," he said, so close above her head that she jerked with surprise. "You even have holes in the lid to admit the sound. Do you mind if I check?"

She held the mike so that he could see her thumb sliding the switch into the "Off" position.

"Ah, the machine is under the floor, of course," he said. "That's right. I . . ."

His hands closed round her neck. She jerked backwards, uselessly. Fury filled her, not at him but at the system that was making him do this, and all the wasted lives, including now her own. She threshed, consciously trying to make it hard for him to find the pressure point, consciously trying to mark her own body so that the struggle would show. Another Lydia, somewhere, longed to be still, to accept, to float into undreaming dark, but she was still writhing against his hard legs and the sink supports and the slithering linoleum when that dark came. In the last instant the hands round her neck, strong and precise, turned into her father's.

184

28

PROCNE'S EYES WERE ROUND as a baby's with horror and
delight. Emotion made her seem yet more fragile and new-
created, just as the first flush of growth in one warm March
week draws out delicate-looking petals which ought to be
completely tender but are, in fact, kitted out by evolution
to stand the tortures of the equinox. In this mood she was
very obviously the daughter of her mother.

"Je-sus!" she whispered. "You sure you're OK? I mean,
you aren't used to it."

All round them the conversations with other prisoners
created privacy.

"I was pretty stiff for a couple of days," admitted Lydia,
not a little smug at her sudden entry into the great sisterhood
of battered women. "My shoulder's not quite right yet, but
otherwise I'm fine. Better than ever, in fact. I almost feel
as if I'd been to a health farm and got toned up."

"I know what you mean. Sometimes a bashing does that
to you, and sometimes it don't. But d'you think he'd actually
have finished you off?"

"I don't know. That's one of the things that's been making
me furious. I've been trying to see him but they won't let
me. They say it's because it's security, but really it's that
bloody little man Austen, getting his own back for my not
telling him about who the man in the coffin was, and your
money, and Mr Ambrose . . ."

"Lucky the police come just then. You ought to count
your blessings, Liz."

"Lucky, my foot! They'd been watching me for weeks,
following me about. I'd even spotted them a couple of
times. And they'd got two men in Mrs Evans's spare room—
I'd noticed she was looking a bit nervous—I think that's
what made me crossest of all, them frightening one of my
own tenants into hiding them so that they could catch me
and Paul making love, or discussing how we'd murdered

your mother, or something, and tiptoeing down and standing outside my door to eavesdrop . . ."

"But honest, Liz, you're lucky they did, or they wouldn't of been there to rush in and haul him off of you. I don't see how you can't see it!"

Lydia laughed.

"That's what Richard says," she said. "*His* chief interest—no, that's not fair, I mean his chief interest after he'd got over worrying about me—is whether the Russians will try to exchange Paul . . ."

"They can't! Not after he's been done for murder!"

"I don't know whether the police can make that stick," said Lydia. "And if they don't there's not much else he can be charged with."

"Bashing you, but—don't tell me—you're not going to bring charges. Honest, Liz, you're just as stupid as the rest of us."

"I expect so. I mean, what's the point? If they don't charge him with murder or something else they'll deport him. That clears him out of *our* lives . . ."

"You'll be sorry, won't you? You liked him?"

"I liked his company. I hated the things he did. And I can't keep them separate. Richard says he has a psychopathic personality. Richard knew quite a lot of spies at one time, and he says four-fifths of them were nut cases. What worries me is that sometimes I'm afraid Dickie's going to grow up like Paul—he lives such a fantasy life. He's inconsolable, poor little brat . . ."

"You didn't tell him!"

"Richard did, as much as he could understand. I shirked it. I was so frightened he'd feel it was my fault, and never forgive me. You see, he'd only just had this other shock of seeing Mr Ambrose beat me up and Paul coming and rescuing me . . ."

Procne frowned, suffering Dickie's lost illusions, his betraying hero. Her sympathy was easy, perhaps even facile, but for the moment it filled her being. Lydia waited for it to seep away, not wanting to mar in any way the news she had been saving up for towards the end of her visit.

"Do you know a vegetarian restaurant called The Organic Traveller?" she said at last.

"I been there," said Procne, suddenly very cautious.

"Well, rather a curious thing happened. While I was talking to Paul I mentioned the name, so it was on my tape which the police took. Besides, they may have heard it when they were listening outside the door. Mr Ambrose's organisation kept their records above the restaurant—I don't know whether you knew?"

Procne shook her head, still wary.

"Well there must have been a leak from the police station, because the organisation started moving their files out. But earlier I'd told a friend of mine about this restaurant, and he works for a local Marxist group . . ."

"Honest, Liz, your friends!"

"He's all right, I think. Listen. He'd been keeping an eye on the place. He didn't explain quite how it happened. I think he'd been planning to fake up a race riot in the restaurant and then hope somehow to get upstairs, but when the van was almost loaded he took his chance—his lot are very efficient—they had a couple of hundred blacks and whites battling up and down in the street—it was all in the papers next day, including that some of the rioters stole a van belonging to a local businessman. My friend's lot are infiltrated by the police of course, so they didn't have very long, but they managed to photocopy a lot of the documents and send them to the *Sunday Times* and the Minister of the Environment and the Director of Public Prosecutions and people like that."

Procne looked appalled.

"Nothing about me!" she whispered. "Not all over again!"

"My friend brought me your file. Some of the others wanted to keep it, but he wouldn't let them even copy it. He's a better bloke than I thought. I burnt it. I hope you don't mind."

"Mind! Me mind! Liz, that's the greatest thing that ever happened! Say, you didn't read it, did you?"

"No. I should have, perhaps, in case there was anything in it that would have been useful to you, but . . . you know, Richard's got about ninety-nine theories about friendship, and one of them is that you've got to accept the face people show you, and not keep looking for faces they don't want you to see. So . . ."

"I only got just the one face," said Procne. "I don't know what you mean, really. This is me."

She looked at Lydia, earnest and puzzled, but also somehow as though she were looking at her own face in a mirror, deciding on the day's make-up. Lydia looked back, thinking that perhaps it was true, perhaps that was the secret of her extraordinary appeal. They both smiled together.

"You know, I feel extraordinarily peaceful," said Lydia. "I feel as though I'd spent the past few weeks walking down a narrow passage whose walls kept getting closer and closer together, all those people trying to lean on me and use me. But now I'm out in the open again."

"Yes, you look like a cat what's . . . oh, Liz, does that mean you've started your baby? My, you can blush, can't you?"

"Hell! The answer is I don't know. I hope so. I've missed a period and I'm pretty regular usually, but it might have been the shock of getting myself strangled and all that."

"Well, where there's hope there's life, like Mum used to say. D'you remember how she used to get that sort of thing inside out?"

"She once told me that wild horses on bended knees wouldn't drag her into some store or other."

"Selfridge's, I bet. She had a thing about Selfridge's, going back to . . ."

They talked, until it was time for Lydia to leave, about that rather awful, rather ordinary old woman who had had so much life in her that even now the memory of her seemed more solid and immediate than any meeting with some living citizen.

"That's what I can't forgive Paul," said Lydia. "Just using her like that, snuffing her out, not knowing what he was doing."

"Don't you worry," said Procne. "He did her a good turn, I been thinking. I mean, where she is now, if she knows it'll be a big thrill, won't it, being a murder victim; even up there there's not a lot of them can say that. And if she don't know, it's no skin off *her* nose, is it? She'd had a smashing life, her way. I mean there wasn't much to it, but she made it smashing, didn't she?"

"Yes. I suppose that's what matters."

"Course it is."